Guess Who's Getting a Party?

In my mind, I could see the invitations I'd hand to my friends next week. I'd cut them in the shape of question marks. Inside, I would write only the date and the time, and tell them to meet at my house.

They would come. I knew my friends well enough to know none of them could resist a mystery . . . or a surprise.

BECKY'S SUPER SECRET

by Carrie Austen

SPLASH™

A BERKLEY / SPLASH BOOK

BECKY'S SUPER SECRET

One

Do you ever wonder where ideas come from?

I have a theory. Some ideas just pop into your head like magic. But others hang around in the back of your mind until something makes them scream *listen to me!* That's what happened with my ideas about grandparents. I'd never thought much about it until—wait, I'm getting ahead of myself.

I guess it really started on the bus one afternoon. Rosie Torres was sitting in the seat in front of Allie and me when she turned around to ask, "Do either of you know what the biology assignment is? I didn't even get what we're supposed to read."

"It's in my notes," Allie answered, making it sound like no big deal. Of course, it probably *wasn't* a big deal for the world's most organized person, Allison Gray. Her spiral notebooks are even color-coordinated with her book covers for each class!

"We have to read chapter eight and list at least ten examples of natural selection," Allie explained.

Rosie leaned over the back of the seat to see Allie's notes. She pointed at the spiral notebook with one of her long peach-colored fingernails. "How do you keep up with everything?"

"It's simple, you just—"

Before Allie could even start her explanation about how she had to be organized because of her big family, Rosie hopped out of her seat. It was her stop. "Okay," Allie said with a laugh. "I can take a hint." We'd all heard her explain it before, and we usually teased her about it.

Rosie smiled as she glanced down at us. "I wish Julie would hurry back from Florida. I miss her." Julie Berger was in the seventh grade with us at Canfield Middle School. Julie, Allie, Rosie, and I spend so much time with one another that my brother sometimes jokes that we're welded together.

After Rosie disappeared down the bus steps, Allie said, "I miss Julie, too. I bet she's having a blast with Goldie."

I looked out the window. "Yeah," I said.

"What's that supposed to mean?" Allie stared at me with her blue eyes.

We all knew Julie was having fun. Who wouldn't love getting out of school for a week? Who wouldn't die for a Florida vacation? As if that weren't enough, Julie was visiting her grandmother, Goldie, who's probably the most fun grandmother on earth.

I sighed. I wasn't sure myself what I meant. My feelings were all mixed up. "It's not like I'm not happy for her, but it doesn't seem fair," I finally told Allie.

"What?" Allie asked. "Not fair that she's in Florida and we're here?"

I pulled Julie's English report out of my folder. (My folders aren't color-coordinated to anything.) With a big sigh, I handed the paper to Allie and said, "It's not fair that Julie never works as hard as we do, and she still got an A."

"An A?" Allie grinned. "Julie got an A? It must be a first. That's great! Why are you upset?"

Slowly, I took my own report out of the folder. When I showed it to Allie, I was careful to hold it so no one else on the bus would see it.

"A C minus!" Allie breathed. "Oh, Becky, you must feel awful!" Getting good grades was really important to me and Allie, and we pretty nearly always got them. So did Rosie, but she just seemed to take it for granted. Julie, though, usually got Bs and Cs, and she couldn't care less. Extracurricular stuff—mostly boys and sports—was Julie's reason for living.

"I read the whole book and wrote a new ending for it, just like Ms. Lombardi told us to do."

"What did Julie do?"

"The same thing." I couldn't help thinking how unfair it was. "Except the book Ms. Lombardi gave her was *Billy McKinley*."

"That's her all-time favorite story!"

"I know."

"Hasn't she read that book over and over again?" Allie asked.

I nodded. "Not to mention that she rented the movie three times. Why couldn't Ms. Lombardi have assigned one of *my* favorite books?"

"Hmm."

Just then Allie had to get off at her stop, and I didn't get to find out what her *hmm* was supposed to mean. Was she agreeing that the assignment was unfair? Or was she telling me to stop feeling sorry for myself?

She had to know I wasn't really mad at Julie. How could I be? Allie, Rosie, Julie and I are a best friend foursome.

But sometimes it's not easy being a friend. Like when you want to be happy because someone else got a good grade, except it's hard because you got a bad grade. Or someone else gets to visit their grandmother, but you can't because you don't have one.

When I got off the bus, I walked down the block and then followed the brick path to the back of my house. The first floor of the building is a restaurant called the Moondance Café—my parents own it. We live upstairs. Unless I want to walk through the big dining room, I go around to the steps in back.

I heard humming as I got close to the door. When I opened it, something smelled great. My mom was baking.

"Are these cookies for us or the restaurant?" I asked her before I grabbed one.

"For us." She laughed. "You know Matthew does the Moondance baking. Russell hasn't let me near the restaurant oven since the day all the cakes fell."

Everyone knows that story. When I was out riding my bike one day, I hit the curb hard and flew off. My mom had to stop mixing a triple recipe of cake batter to bandage my knee, and when she finally got back to the kitchen, she forgot to add the baking powder. The finished cakes looked more like pancakes! It was really just a coincidence that Matthew, our new pastry chef, was scheduled to start the very next day, but ever since then my stepdad has been teasing my mom about how we can't let her near the restaurant oven. Anyway, Matthew bakes all the Moondance's desserts now.

"It wasn't your fault," I told her. "Anyone can make a mistake."

"Speak for yourself, Becky 'Butterfingers' Bartlett."

I blushed. I'm used to my older brother David calling me a walking disaster. But my mom?

She gave me a hug. It was an unspoken apology.

"You have mail," she said as if she had just remembered. "It's on the hall table."

Mail? I never get mail. Something good was finally happening after a completely crummy day.

But when I saw the postcard showing a sunny, beautiful beach, my heart sank. Who did I know at the beach except Julie?

I picked it up, but I didn't read it until I had flopped into the big, overstuffed chair in the living room. Julie had made her neat handwriting small to fit all her news on the card. It said, "You won't believe it! Goldie introduced me to the cutest guy. And I won $25 at bingo! See you soon (I'll be the one with the tan). Love, Julie."

I threw the card across the room and tried to sort out my feelings. I wasn't jealous about the cute boy. Julie is boy-crazy. So is Rosie. But neither Allie nor I can get real excited about any guys yet. My mother says it will happen for us sometime.

No, it wasn't the cute boy. I wouldn't mind tan-ning on a great beach somewhere, but mostly I wanted a grandmother like Goldie. She sent Julie fun cards and even better presents; she called once or twice a week and always listened, ready with sympathy and good advice; she even told great funny stories.

My mother's father died when she was fifteen, and her mother died when I was a baby. I don't know much about Russell's parents, either, except that they died before he met my mom. There was no one like Goldie for me.

Maybe it was too much to want someone exactly like Goldie, I thought. I really just wanted someone who'd always think I was special—someone who'd always be special to me. Was that too much to ask?

Don't get me wrong. I love my mom and Russell. I even love my pain-in-the-neck older brother, David. And I know they love me (although sometimes it's *extremely* hard to tell with David). But grandparents are different.

Sometimes I wonder what things would be like if my real dad hadn't left us just before I was born. I mean, Russell is a great guy and everything, but still . . .

"Did Julie have any interesting news?" my mother asked.

I hadn't seen her come into the room. "Didn't you read it?"

"Of course not." She picked up the card and handed it back to me. "I wouldn't read your mail."

"But you knew it was from Julie."

"I recognized her handwriting," she explained.

That made sense. "Well, she's having a great time in Florida. Of course."

"I bet you miss her."

"We all miss her. Especially since we have a party to plan for a week from Saturday."

"A party *and* a week's worth of school to catch up on?" My mom shook her head as if she were glad she wasn't Julie. "She's going to be one busy girl."

The last thing I wanted to talk about was Julie's schoolwork. It just reminded me of her lucky A—and my miserable C minus.

"Well, at least she'll be well rested for it," I said. I couldn't help the sarcastic tone that crept into my voice as I said it. Then I caught my mom staring at me in this special way she has, with her head tilted to one side. It usually means she's wondering if it's okay to laugh, or if she should sit down for a long talk about what's bothering you.

I didn't feel like having a long talk, so I put my thumbs in my ears, wiggled my fingers, and stuck my tongue out at her. She burst out laughing and came over and ruffled my hair.

"Becky, when Russell and I start planning our next family vacation, I'll make sure sunny beaches are included on the itinerary. After all, you need your rest, too!"

"Thanks, Mom," I said. Silently I added, *and do you think you could include grandparents, too?*

Two

The party I'd told my mom we had to plan was a birthday party for seven-year-old Josh Stevenson, and we'd learned about it three hours after Julie's plane left for Florida. While Julie was only one-fourth of The Party Line, we couldn't do much planning until she came back, since we do our best work as a team.

The Party Line is really a fun business. It all started when the birthday party for Allie's little brother fell apart at the last minute. The clown Mrs. Gray had hired didn't show up, and when we all stopped by looking to glom some of the extra birthday cake, the Gray house was a disaster area. The horde of disappointed four-year-olds was ready to start the nursery school equivalent of a riot, so we decided to pitch in. Rosie started drawing faces on balloons, and I did dumb magic tricks with Allie as my assistant. The kids had a great time, and their parents were really impressed. Well, one parent talked to another, and the next thing we knew, someone wanted to hire us to do a party for her six-year-old. The Party Line was born.

Running a business—even a party business—is *not* easy. Allie, the organized one, takes care of filling out an information sheet for each party so we don't forget anything—she's vice-president. Rosie's the best in math, so she's our treasurer. Their work helps us decide how much to charge for each party: enough to cover our expenses plus profit for us. Julie's the secretary, and I'm president, because I came up with the idea of starting a party business.

To keep the business from interfering with school, we hold our regular meeting on Sunday afternoon in my attic. Of course, we can always talk about little details and things on the bus or during lunch any day.

Julie would not get home until very late Sunday night, though, so this week just Allie, Rosie, and I would be getting together in my attic. I wondered how the meeting would work without Julie. At least there would be three of us.

The next day at lunch, I nearly choked on my applesauce when Allie said, "Uh, B-Becky?" She only stammers when she's nervous. And since there was nothing in the entire lunchroom to worry her, I could only guess she had really bad news. I hoped she wasn't going to tell me the math test had been rescheduled for that afternoon instead of the next day.

"What's wrong?" I asked. If it was bad news, I had to hear it sometime. Waiting wouldn't make it sound any better.

"I can't come to the meeting Sunday afternoon."

If she couldn't come, it would be just Rosie and me. I didn't know how Rosie felt, but I didn't think the two of us could plan the party alone. "Why not?"

"I have to visit my grandmother."

I almost fell off my chair. "You're going away, too?" I yelped. Allie's grandmother lived in Pennsylvania.

"No, she's moving into Pine Villa," Allie said. "The day after tomorrow."

"That's neat!" Pine Villa was a retirement complex close to Allie's house. She could see her grandmother every day! "Aren't you excited?"

Allie thought for a minute. "I guess."

She didn't sound too enthusiastic. Obviously she didn't think this was great news, like I did. If I had a grandmother at Pine Villa I'd be doing cartwheels. I'd visit her so often that my mom would think I'd moved in with her.

"Anyway," Allie said, interrupting my thoughts, "she's moving into her new apartment this weekend. We're all helping out, so I'll be there Saturday morning, unpacking. Ugh. Then on Sunday we're all going over at noon for the whole day. It's sort of a family housewarming party."

Rosie, who was sitting next to me, played with her gold hoop earrings. "Why don't we meet Sunday morning? About eleven?"

"We can't. This Sunday is the first day my parents are serving brunch at the Moondance," I reminded her.

"I guess they don't want us tromping through the restaurant. We might bother the customers." Rosie, as usual, was very understanding, but this time she was wrong.

"We haven't upset anyone since the time we tried the player piano in the attic." I smiled when I remembered that day. We hadn't expected the old piano to work, but it had, booming so loudly that all the dishes downstairs rattled. "No, we can't meet Sunday morning because I have to work."

"There's a salad bar at brunch?" Allie asked. "So people can make bacon, lettuce, and tomato sandwiches if they want?" Allie knew that my usual job was keeping the salad bar stocked.

"I'm going to be helping Russell in the kitchen." I smiled because I was truly proud my parents were giving me a chance to do something important.

"Near the hot ovens and sharp knives and boiling water?" Allie asked, astonished.

I sighed. My friends knew too much about my

klutz attacks. "They don't really have a choice. Most of the college kids who work for us are taking the weekend off to study for midterms."

Rosie shivered. "Don't even mention midterms."

Allie nodded grimly. Our own midterms were not far away, and we had an unspoken agreement to avoid talking about them until it was absolutely necessary.

"Wait a minute!" When Rosie smiled, her dark eyes sparkled. "Sunday's not the only day we can meet. We could do it Saturday afternoon instead."

I shook my head. "Not this weekend. My brother has a track meet."

The meeting dilemma was forgotten temporarily. Allie's mouth fell open. "David? Running track?"

I giggled. "Hard to imagine, isn't it? He's trying to impress one of the waitresses at the Moondance."

Rosie grinned, and her dark eyes were laughing, too. "You mean David has it bad for a *college* girl?" Everyone knew that all the waiters and waitresses at the Moondance were from Taylor College.

"And she ignores him." I smiled, thinking about David staring at the girl night after night. "It's taken thirteen years, but I'm finally getting to see my brother make a fool of himself."

"Is he any good at track?" Allie asked.

I laughed so loudly that people from the next table turned to look at me. "He comes home every night with aching feet. He tried to tell me he held the record for the hurdles."

"The record for taking the longest to finish the event?" Allie guessed.

Rosie shook her dark hair out of her face. "I bet it was the record for knocking over the most hurdles."

"Isn't it dumb? He's doing it all for a girl who couldn't care less."

"Mmm." Rosie's dark eyes turned dreamy. "I think it's kind of romantic."

Allie and I exchanged looks. "I don't get it," Allie said. "Are you going to the meet?"

"No, but I'm filling in for him at the Moondance because while he's at the meet we'll be shorthanded."

Allie finished her sandwich. "What about after the track meet? About four o'clock? I should be done unpacking my grandma's ten thousand photographs by then."

"My parents expect me to work at four-thirty." I'd be doing my regular job chopping vegetables and making sure we don't run out of anything during the evening rush. If I must say so myself, I do it well. I haven't cut off any fingers with the big knife, and no one seems worried about me dropping lettuce all over the floor when I fill the salad bar bowls in public. Of course, David was betting it would happen before the end of the month.

There had to be another time for our meeting. "I don't have to hang around the Moondance until closing, though. Can you both come over after dinner Saturday night? I'll make some popcorn—"

This time Rosie said, "Not me. I'm going to the symphony with my parents."

"The symphony?" In fifth grade our music class took a field trip to the Canfield Symphony Orchestra. I fell asleep. Or I would have, except for all the noise.

Rosie shrugged her shoulders. "It's a benefit thing. I'll survive."

Maybe Rosie would be fine, but I was getting worried. It was starting to look like I'd be the only one at the weekly Party Line meeting. "Let's go over this one more time. What's happening Saturday morning?"

"My grandmother," Allie answered.

"Saturday afternoon is David's track meet and my job at the Moondance," I said, filling in my part of the schedule. "And Saturday night—"

"The symphony." Rosie grinned.

I sighed. Saturday was out of the question. "Sunday morning is the brunch, and after that—"

"The housewarming at Pine Villa," Allie finished for me.

"And Sunday night?" When no one said they had tons of homework or some family thing, I held my breath.

"I can come over to your house after dinner," Allie volunteered.

Rosie nodded. "Me, too."

"Great!" We'd finally solved the meeting problem.

"But I have to be home by nine," Rosie added. She had a curfew on school nights. "That gives us about two hours to plan the party."

"The whole party?" Allie asked. "Shouldn't we wait for Julie?"

"We'll never be ready for the party if we wait until next week to start planning it!" I was sure Julie was lying on some Florida beach right at that moment and couldn't care less about The Party Line.

Rosie turned serious. "She's right. We can decide on the theme, though, and make up a basic checklist of supplies. That will still leave a lot for Julie to help with when she gets back."

"Sounds good!" I was glad we had settled things. Now I wanted to hear more about Allie's grandmother. I told her, "I bet the housewarming will be fun."

"I don't know. Can you imagine all my brothers and sisters squeezed into some little apartment?"

"Not Jonathan." Her four-year-old brother was full of energy. It seemed like he was always getting into some kind of trouble. Not bad trouble—just little kid trouble. He could probably manage to bounce off the walls in a football stadium.

"Grandma is pretty patient. She never seems to get mad at him," Allie said.

"Tell me more about her." Suddenly I was full of curiosity about Allie's grandmother. Maybe if she told me enough about her grandma, it would make up for my not having one of my own.

"Well, one of the best things is that she tells great stories about when my mom was little," Allie said with a grin. "Do you believe *my* mother once climbed an apple tree to rescue a kitten? And then she panicked, fell out of the tree, and broke her arm!"

"Your mom?" I was amazed. Mrs. Gray always seems so cool and collected. It was impossible to imagine her ever losing control, even as a kid.

"And she cried for days when she couldn't understand fractions," Allie told us.

Rosie laughed. Math was easy for her. "Your mom cried over fractions?"

Allie nodded. "And now she helps me with my math homework all the time. She says she never wants me to worry about math the way she did. My grandmother always told her not to worry, too. But Grandma says the one thing that never changed is that my mother always tried to stay on top of everything. And she was always a worrywart."

Rosie and I looked at each other and burst out laughing. "Now we know where Allie gets it," Rosie giggled. Allie put her hands on her hips and tried to look tough. But her big grin gave her away. "My grandmother says the same thing," she finally admitted, prompting a whole new round of hilarity among the three of us.

Allie's grandmother sounded like fun. I wished I had a grandparent, someone to tell me neat things about the past. And I wouldn't mind being spoiled the way Goldie treats Julie, either.

The bell rang and we hurried to put all our trash in the garbage cans. We were almost out of the lunchroom when Rosie turned to Allie. "What happened to the kitten? The one that was stuck in the tree?"

Allie laughed. "After my mom was rushed to the doctor the kitten crawled down the tree trunk all by itself!"

Three

"What do we know about Josh Stevenson?" I said, starting off the meeting on Sunday night. After all, I was the president of The Party Line.

The three of us were in my attic. Even before we started The Party Line, we had cleaned out a big space in the middle of the attic for our private clubhouse. Allie was reclining on a giant purple pillow, and Rosie was sitting on a small Oriental carpet. I sat leaning back against an ancient dresser, and hoped the torn lampshades balanced on top of it wouldn't fall on my head.

"Josh Stevenson." Rosie tapped her pen against a pad of lined paper. With Julie gone, she was our temporary secretary.

Allie started to count off the facts on her fingers. "He's turning seven and he's in first grade. He's the youngest child in his family." Leave it to Allie to have a dossier on the kid.

"Does he like dinosaurs?" Rosie asked.

"Don't all little boys?" I thought about Allie's youngest brother, Jonathan, also known as Mouse. He loves dinosaurs and can name practically every species. I bet he knows more about them than Ms. Pernell, our biology teacher.

Allie checked her notes. "No. Josh loves monsters and other scary, disgusting things."

"How do you know all that?" I exploded at Allie.

Allie and I have been best friends practically forever. So she doesn't even blink anymore at my outbursts. After all, she knows I don't mean anything by it. "You're just the excitable type," she always tells me. Now she looked up at me calmly and said, "Becky, if you ever bothered to read all the way through the information sheet, you'd see a space for stuff like this. I just called Mrs. Stevenson and asked her." Then she grinned at me.

She was right, of course. I just didn't have the patience to go through the whole form, and I certainly didn't have brain space to waste remembering it all. That's what the form was for, so you could just read through it when you took a business call, asking the client each question in order. Naturally, my friends made sure I hardly ever had to take Party Line calls by putting my number last on the flyer. I guess they did it partly because I'm the busiest what with working part-time at the Moondance—and partly because, well, that sort of detail wasn't something I exactly excelled at.

"What can we do for a seven year old who loves monsters?" Rosie mused.

"Monsters? Maybe we could use David as a prop," I teased.

Allie laughed, but Rosie just smiled. She was sketching something on her notepad. It looked like the minutes of our meeting were going to be illustrated.

"What *is* it?" Allie wrinkled her nose at Rosie. I inched closer to the notepad to see what I was missing. At first I thought it was a man's head. But what kind of man had an eye in the middle of his forehead? Or huge pointed ears?

Rosie looked up, her dangling earrings jingling. She grinned and announced, "It's a monster. I'm trying to get into the mood."

"Right." Suddenly, Allie hooked her fingers inside each corner of her mouth and pulled her lips into an ugly grimace. She grunted and said something that sounded like, "Uh-uh uh uh uh-uh."

"What? Are you trying to tell us something, Allie?"

Her fingers came out of her mouth with a pop. "Can't you understand monster talk?"

Rosie giggled. "I guess not."

Uh-uh uh uh uh-uh. I played back Allie's monster

talk inside my head. It had the right number of syllables to be "Happy Birthday to you," but if we walked around Josh's party talking in grunts no one would understand anything we were saying.

I was confused. "What if I don't want to walk around the party with my hands in my mouth?"

Allie giggled. "I didn't mean we should. That would be gross! I was just trying to get into a monstery mood, like Rosie. Come on, Becky, let out the monster in you."

They both looked at me, expecting me to do something weird. I didn't feel very creative—or very monstery. I scrunched up one eye and pulled down my lower lip.

"I'm not scared," Allie said critically.

"But it *is* disgusting," Rosie told her. She tugged the sleeves of her soft magenta sweater over her wrists. The warm color looked great with her black hair. Next to her, I had to look pretty boring in my sweats. But I'd worked the brunch shift as well as the dinner rush, and I had wanted to be comfortable. Of course, Rosie even looks good in sweats.

"Are you done making faces?" Allie asked me.

I crossed my eyes and said, "Sure. Let's get to work on this monster bash."

"Monster bash?" Rosie groaned.

"I like it!" Allie cried.

Rosie thought about it for a moment, then waved

her pen in the air. "It'll work if we can come up with some monster games."

I tried to think of the Halloween parties I had gone to, and some my mom had held for David at home. "There's one game where you blindfold everyone and make them guess what they're touching."

"What *are* they touching?" Rosie's pen was ready to write as soon as I told her some more.

I closed my eyes and tried to remember. The first thing that came back to me was the feeling of worms slithering slimily between my fingers. "Cold, wet spaghetti!"

"You want to make the boys touch some spaghetti?" Allie rolled her eyes. "That's not scary. It's messy. Those boys are going to laugh us right out of the house."

"No, no, no." She wasn't getting the right idea. I tried to explain it better. "You blindfold the boys, make them stick their hands into a bowl of cold, wet spaghetti, and make them guess what it is."

"And the winner gets a prize?" Rosie asked.

Haven't they been to any good Halloween parties? I wondered. "You guys, it feels really gross and slimy. Like worms or snakes. After they all guess things like that, you dare them to eat it."

"Ooh." Allie clapped her hands. "I'm going to try that on Mouse if he ever puts sand in my bed again."

"You are positively grim." Rosie tossed her dark

hair over her shoulders and leaned toward me. "Do you have any more ideas?"

"Peeled grapes," I told them. When they both glanced at me, I smiled. "They feel like eyeballs."

Allie got a crooked grin on her face. "So big grapes would feel like monster eyeballs."

"And cottage cheese . . ." I waited.

"Would feel like brains!" Allie and Rosie chimed in.

"What about making the boys into monsters? I could paint their faces." Rosie's pen was speeding across the paper. "And we could bring lots of weird things with us and see who could make the best monster costume out of them."

"Like rubber noses and warts?" I asked.

Rosie waved her well-manicured fingers in the air. "And fake fingernails."

Allie bounced up and down on her purple pillow. "What if we kept a big pot of boiling water on the stove? Like we were brewing something nasty?"

"We wouldn't even need to boil something—it would be dangerous in case one of the boys bumped into the pot and it spilled. We could use dry ice to make the vapor. I can get some," I volunteered.

"So what would be in the pot?" Allie asked.

"Monster potion," Rosie said in a deep, throaty croak.

"We could hide a pitcher inside the pot and pour

the potion—I mean the punch—into their cups when we serve the cake," I said, loving the idea. The kids wouldn't know it was just punch, and I wondered how many seven-year-old boys would actually taste it. They would probably dare each other to be the first one to take a sip.

"What if we strung a big spiderweb over the table?" Allie asked. She was really getting into the monster theme.

"Only if it has creepy *things* in it," Rosie decided.

"This is going to be great!" I knew we wouldn't do anything to really scare the kids. But they were going to have a wonderful time at the monster bash.

"I hope the boys have half as much fun as we're having today," Allie said.

Rosie frowned. "It's too bad Julie isn't here. She's missing all the good parts."

"Yeah." Allie sighed. "Not to mention *we're* missing out on all her good ideas. But she'll be here when we figure out the rest of the details."

"She'd better be." The others looked at me, and I felt my face get hot.

I hadn't meant to sound mean, but I just couldn't feel sorry for Julie. No one was holding her hostage in Florida. Meanwhile, we were short-handed. It wasn't easy to run a business, go to school, and do chores and homework. Plus I had to help out at the Moondance. (True, I get paid for that—but I really earn it.) Julie was part of the business. I could understand that she'd prefer a week in Florida with her grandmother over staying home to attend our meeting. Still, I wasn't going to worry about her because she'd missed our fun monster session.

"I didn't mean it that way," I said. "It's just that we'll really need all four of us to do this party." I didn't want to try to explain the real reason I felt upset with Julie. She just seemed to have everything I wanted: a vacation in Florida, an A on her English paper, and a grandmother.

Speaking of grandmothers, I suddenly remembered where Allie had been before our meeting. "How was the housewarming party at Pine Villa?" I asked.

"It was pretty fun." Allie pointed to a teeny-tiny purplish spot on her shirt. "But Mouse tripped over my foot and when his blueberry pie flew into the air some of it landed on me."

I didn't want to hear about flying pieces of pie. I wanted to know about Allie's grandma. "What's her name?"

"My grandmother?" Allie seemed surprised by my question. "Cecilia."

Cecilia. It gave me a whole different feeling than the name Goldie did. Julie's grandmother acted like a Goldie—she went places and did exciting things. But Cecilia sounded old-fashioned and beautiful.

"What's she like?"

"She's short. Almost as short as me." Allie smiled. She is the shortest of our foursome, and everyone knows she wants to be taller.

"Is she pretty?" I asked, trying to get a picture of her in my mind.

Allie shrugged. "Her hair is white and she wears glasses. But I've seen some old photos. Her hair was dark and really curly. And she had the neatest smile. There are pictures of her when she was young where she looks like an old-fashioned movie star."

"I bet your grandmother has a lot of great old photographs," said Rosie.

Allie laughed. "You wouldn't think they were so great if *you* had to unpack and arrange all ten zillion of them," she said, rolling her eyes. "Some of them *are* pretty neat, though. There's one of my mom when she was Mouse's age, and she's missing both her front teeth. And there are some of people wearing really funny old-fashioned clothes—especially my great-grandparents."

I had the strangest feeling. It was like an ache in my heart. I didn't even have a grandmother, but Allie knew what her *great*-grandparents looked like!

"The next time you visit your grandmother, can I go with you?" I asked Allie.

"Why?" She squinted at me.

"Really," Rosie added, snapping the top of her felt-tip pen. "Why do you want to meet Allie's grandma?"

"Because she sounds neat." For some reason, I couldn't tell them I wanted to meet Allie's grandmother because I didn't have any grandparents of my own. They would have laughed. But I needed to share Allie's grandma for a while.

"I'm going to run errands for her a few times a week," Allie said. "You can come along if you really want to, but Pine Villa is kind of depressing. I mean, everyone there is so *old*."

And special, I thought to myself. "When do you think you'll be doing your first errand?"

"I'm not sure. She'll call us if she needs something."

"And you'll call me?" I wanted to be sure she really would remember to pick me up on her way to Pine Villa.

"Sure."

Allie raised her eyebrows in Rosie's direction and Rosie shrugged. They thought I was crazy. What did they know about the empty feeling next to my heart?

Four

"Thanks for inviting me," I told Allie on our way to Pine Villa after dinner Monday evening. "I was surprised when you called—you were at your grandmother's just yesterday."

"I didn't think I'd be going back so soon, either. Here, hold this," Allie said, handing me a brown paper bag so she could reclip a barrette that had come loose. "My mom baked a cake for dessert, and she wanted Grandma to have some. I'm the designated errand person."

I handed her back the bag as we crossed the street and stepped onto Pine Villa's sidewalk. My heart started beating faster as we got closer to the front door. I don't usually get all choked up about things. But I was really excited—and really nervous and kind of scared—about meeting Allie's grandmother.

"We're here to see Mrs. Laporte," Allie told the woman behind the desk. While the receptionist punched buttons on her phone, Allie leaned close to me and whispered, "It's so quiet in here. It's worse than the library!" The ticking of the clock behind the desk was the loudest sound in the lobby, but I could barely hear it because of the noise of the blood pounding in my ears.

The woman hung up and smiled at us. "Your grandmother is anxious to see you. Go right on up."

Did the receptionist think Mrs. Laporte was my grandmother, too? What would it feel like if I were waiting in the lobby to see my very own grandmother or grandfather?

Stop it, Bartlett, I told myself sternly. I had to get tough, or else I was going to start feeling sorry for myself. And I wanted to have a good time with Allie's grandma.

I followed Allie across a carpet that muffled our footsteps. The Pine Villa living room was just as quiet as the lobby. Compared to all the noise at the Moondance, I thought the silence was wonderful.

We took an elevator to the third floor. Mrs. Laporte's apartment was halfway down the hall.

She must have been watching for Allie through the peephole because the door opened before we could knock. A small, white-haired woman met us with a smile. "Allison, I'm so happy to see you." She stretched out her arms, pulling Allie into a hug. Allie kissed her grandmother on the cheek.

"Who is this?" Mrs. Laporte asked. She tipped her

glasses down her nose and peered over the top of them.

"Grandma, this is my friend, Becky Bartlett."

"Hello, Becky." Mrs. Laporte gave me the same warm smile she had shown Allie. It made me grin in return.

She took Allie by the hand and started to pull her through the door. "Come on in, kids. I hope you like chocolate chips—I have a whole bunch of cookies and some cold milk waiting for you." Cookies and milk! It sounded so grandmotherly.

"They're our favorite!" Allie gave her grandmother a quick hug, then bounced into the living room. I followed her, looking at the cozy room. It was all pink. The carpet was dusty rose, and the small sofa and a chair were covered in a deep rose floral fabric. The walnut tables at either end of the sofa were covered with lacy runners and framed photographs.

Allie followed her grandmother into the tiny kitchen off the living room. "I brought you some cake Mom baked," Allie said, handing over the paper bag. Allie's grandmother set the bag down on the counter and took a carton of milk from the refrigerator. "Thank you, dear. I'll eat it tomorrow. Here, would you bring these napkins and the cookies into the living room?"

Allie came back into the living room and put the

napkins and cookies on the dark, polished coffee table. "Isn't this a really nice apartment?" she said to me.

I pointed to the pictures and figurines on the tables and the small desk in the corner. "It looks like your grandmother has lived here forever. It's hard to believe she just moved in over the weekend."

"We all worked really hard. My job was dusting all the picture frames and the ceramic birds. It took absolutely *forever*!"

I picked up a framed picture. "Who's this?"

Allie leaned over to get a look at it. "It's my grandma and grandpa's wedding."

I studied the old photograph. They both looked so happy and so young. It was hard to imagine that the woman holding the bouquet of lilies in the picture was the same person in the kitchen.

Suddenly I felt so rude. I jumped to my feet and called, "Mrs. Laporte, can I help you?"

"Why, thank you, Becky." I stepped into the kitchen and she handed me two full glasses. She smiled a little ruefully. "I'm afraid I'm a little shaky sometimes these days. I know *you* won't spill the milk."

"I'll try not to, but I'm subject to klutz attacks," I warned her.

She stopped and looked at me. *Really* looked at

me. When she finished checking me out, she said, "Nonsense. You're a fine, healthy young lady."

I smiled. I liked the way she called me a *young lady*.

Allie came up behind me and reached for her grandmother's cup of coffee. "Grandma, you should listen to Becky. Believe me, I know how easy it is for her to break stuff."

Mrs. Laporte just smiled as if she knew Allie was wrong about me. Then she went into the living room and lowered herself into one of the chairs.

We settled back into our spots on the sofa. Allie bit into a cookie and sighed. She really loved chocolate chips. "Did you make these, Grandma?"

"Heavens, no. I'm still too discombobulated by the move to start a baking project." She winked at me as I took a second cookie. "But I will soon."

"I bet you make the best chocolate chip cookies," I told her.

Allie shook her head. "Grandma's specialty is oatmeal-raisin. My mom uses the same recipe." I'd eaten those cookies at Allie's house. They were terrific—and I don't usually like raisins. I thought about all the stuff my mom bakes, like cookies and bread and muffins. Were any of those recipes handed down from her mother?

"Grandma, where *did* you get these cookies?" Allie asked. "They can't be store-bought. They're too good."

Mrs. Laporte looked pleased. "One of my new neighbors gave them to me to welcome me to Pine Villa."

"It's great that you have such friendly neighbors, Mrs. Laporte," I said.

"I know I'm old," Mrs. Laporte said with a sparkle in her eye, "but too much formality makes me feel positively ancient. So, Becky, why don't you just call me Grandma instead of Mrs. Laporte?"

I couldn't believe it, but I was thrilled. "Uh . . . okay," I stammered.

"Unless you save that name for your own grandmother," Mrs. Laporte added.

"No, uh, I don't have a grandmother," I said quietly.

Allie stared at me. She started to open her mouth but her grandmother put a hand on her arm.

"Well, then, that's settled," Mrs. Laporte said. "Right, Becky?"

"Right, Mrs.—uh, Grandma," I said. I felt wildly happy.

"You know, I think you girls would like Miss Laura," Mrs. Laporte said.

"Who's Miss Laura?" Allie asked.

"Why don't you come downstairs with me and find out?" Mrs. Laporte said mysteriously, getting up from her chair. "She should be downstairs in the community room right now."

"Let's go!" I carried my milk glass into the kitchen and washed it in the sink. What kind of person would be called Miss Laura?

Allie slipped her glass next to mine under the faucet. "Why are you so excited?" she asked softly.

"Aren't you curious about this Miss Laura?"

"Not really." We set our glasses in the drying rack on the counter. Then Allie explained, "Because my grandmother used to live so far away, I never used to see her a lot. It's hard enough knowing what to say to her. But what are we going to do in the community room with a bunch of strangers?"

Mrs. Laporte slipped her key off the hook by the door and dropped it into her skirt pocket. As Allie and I came out of the kitchen, she looked at us expectantly.

It looked like we were going to meet Miss Laura whether Allie wanted to or not. I nudged her with my elbow. "Trust me. It'll be fun."

Allie rolled her eyes. She wasn't convinced.

The community room seemed to be where most of Pine Villa's residents hung out. Some people were watching television in the corner. A card game was going on at one of the tables. In the center of the room, comfortable couches and chairs were arranged in little conversation groups.

Allie's grandmother led us to the middle of the room, where a deep-voiced woman sat in the center of a group. The men and women seated near her were all leaning forward to listen to her.

"Chicago in the twenties was not to be believed," she was saying. "I barely got out of the Diamond Club alive."

Mrs. Laporte whispered, "That's Miss Laura."

Miss Laura was striking. Her smooth white hair was drawn back and gathered by a clip at the nape of her neck. Her dark eyes sparkled almost as much as the dozens of bright glass beads cascading from her neck to her waist. She was tall and thin, and she sat straight on the edge of a sofa, her long fingers gesturing gracefully as she spoke. She was wearing a long cobalt blue silk tunic over skinny black silk pants. Embroidered gold Chinese slippers glittered on her feet as she recrossed her legs.

I grabbed a chair from another furniture group and pulled it into Miss Laura's circle for Allie's grandmother. Allie and I sat on the floor on either side.

"Hello, Cecilia," Miss Laura interrupted herself to say. "Who are your guests?"

Mrs. Laporte rested her hand on Allie's shoulder. "This is my granddaughter, Allison." Then she turned to me. "And this is her friend, Becky Bartlett."

"What do you girls know about Chicago?" Miss Laura boomed. She was a big woman with a big voice to match.

"Nothing." The only place I knew much about was Canfield, Vermont. "Are you from Chicago?" I asked.

Her laugh was deep and throaty. "I'm from lots of places. But I grew up in Boston . . . and stayed there until my father disinherited me."

"Disinherited you!" My mouth fell open. Allie's blue eyes were wide.

"He said I could be a showgirl if that's what I wanted. But if I left, he didn't want to see me in his house ever again." Miss Laura didn't blink telling the story. You could tell she wasn't one bit sorry.

"You were a sh-showgirl?" Allie blurted. Miss Laura fastened her gaze on Allie, and my best friend's face grew pink. Allie hung her head. I knew how much she hated it when she began to stutter.

"The best the Chicago Follies ever saw." Miss Laura grinned. "And I went all over the country, too, singing and dancing in a traveling revue. Is that hard to believe?"

"Do you still sing?" I asked.

The man in the next chair laughed. "Every chance she gets. Sometimes we have to pay her to stop!"

From her spot in the chair, Mrs. Laporte said with a laugh in her voice, "I don't believe you, Max."

His dark eyes were twinkling when he told Allie's grandmother, "No one ever does. None of my students ever believed me, either. Why should things change now?"

Had he been a teacher? I was sure that every person in the room had done something exciting when he or she was younger. But had they ever expected to end up together? Take Max. Had he ever dreamed he'd be spending his evenings with a retired showgirl? I wanted to know more about him. "Where did you teach, uh, Mr. Max?"

"High school, right here in Canfield. And plain Max will do."

"We go to Canfield Middle School," Allie told him.

"And we'll be at the high school in two years . . . if we're lucky." I tapped myself on the head. "Knock on wood."

Allie giggled. "You'll make it, Becky. You're one of the best students."

"Tell that to Ms. Lombardi and my C minus."

"You just need to study," Max told us. "That's what I used to tell Sandy Lombardi."

"You know Ms. Lombardi!" Allie and I exclaimed in unison.

He nodded. "Sandy studied hard, but even so she

got Cs of her own once in a while. Had the most beautiful long golden braids, though."

Allie and I stared at each other. Ms. Lombardi wore long golden braids! And I knew we were thinking the same thing: Who else did he know?

Max rubbed his chin. "So, you have Sandy Lombardi for a teacher. My, my. I wonder if you girls know any of my other students?"

Allie and I laughed. "We were wondering if you knew any of our other teachers," I said shyly.

"Well, one of my most memorable students was Franny Newman, but she didn't go on to teach," Max said.

"Who was Franny Newman?" I wondered if she was somebody famous. Maybe she was an actress.

"Franny was a wonderful student and a very nice girl," he told us. "What I remember best is Franny's mother. She used to chaperone some of the school dances." He chuckled. "I don't know who had more fun at the parties, the kids or Goldie."

Allie's hand flew to her mouth. And I grinned so hard my face hurt. Mrs. Berger's first name was Franny. He was talking about her and about Julie's grandmother, Goldie!

"Do you girls know Goldie?" Max asked.

"We've never met her, but we've heard about her," I tried to explain. "She's our friend's grandmother."

Miss Laura laughed. "The famous Goldie is your friend's grandma? And Cecilia here is your grandma?" she asked Allie.

"Yes." Allie looked up at her grandmother, and Mrs. Laporte reached down and put her hand on Allie's shoulder.

"What about you, Becky?" Miss Laura continued. She glanced around the room as though she were looking for someone. "Who's your grandmother?"

I knew Miss Laura was just being friendly and curious, but her question still hurt. Softly, I told her, "I don't have one."

Miss Laura looked at me like she had heard the sadness in my voice. "That's not right," she declared. "Every young person should have a grandma. And everyone my age should have a granddaughter."

"Do you?" I asked boldly. "Do you have grandchildren?"

Miss Laura let out a sigh. "No." Then she brightened. "Not unless you'll let me adopt you."

"Adopt me?"

"It wouldn't be anything official, of course," Miss Laura went on. "But if you ever feel like visiting your grandma, you can come and see me."

"Wow! You wouldn't mind?"

Miss Laura seemed pleased and surprised. "I *never* say anything I don't mean," she said emphatically.

"Will you tell me stories about Chicago in the twenties?" I asked eagerly.

"Will I?" Miss Laura laughed. "Becky, everyone around here is bored to tears with my old stories. I'd love a new audience. I'll tell you stories as long as you want to hear them."

This was great! "Do you think you could bake me some chocolate chip cookies?" I asked hopefully.

"Baking was never a talent of mine," she said. "But I could teach you a few songs."

"You don't want to learn any of her songs," Max warned me. "I can see you're going to need some help if Miss Laura's going to be your grandmother. I guess I'll have to be your adopted granddad."

"Max!" Miss Laura leaned over and grasped his hand playfully. "Does this mean we're engaged?"

He grinned. "My father told me never to marry a showgirl."

Everyone in the room laughed. Allie and I looked at each other and started to giggle. Deep down inside I was blissfully happy. Not only had I acquired a pair of adoptive grandparents, but it seemed as though I had become the second banana in a runaway vaudeville act!

Five

"Can you believe it? He knows Goldie!" Allie told Julie the next afternoon. We were on our way to the Pine Tree Mall for our party shopping.

"Who'd ever believe you could have such a good time at Pine Villa?" Julie asked, running her hand through her short honey-blond hair. After Rosie had tried to trim it and had accidentally cut off too much, we'd never thought Julie would get used to it. But now she loves her hair short.

"I sure wouldn't have if Becky hadn't come with me last night. She didn't have any trouble talking to the old people," Allie said.

"Don't talk about me like I'm not here," I teased them. "Sooner or later you would have found out about Max and Goldie . . . and Ms. Lombardi's braids."

"No kidding, Ms. Lombardi wore *braids*?" Rosie stopped short.

"Long *golden* braids," Allie added.

"I just can't believe it," Rosie said.

"This is fascinating, but I'm hungry!" Julie grinned. She's always hungry. "When can we eat?"

"There's some soda and pretzels and stuff at my house," I told them. "We have to get our shopping done fast so we can go home and invent disgusting party games."

"She's right." Rosie opened the door and held it for me. "I've been trying to think of ideas for disgusting games for the past couple of days, but I haven't been having much luck."

"Oh, I've got some really sick ideas," I said, not thinking about what I was saying. Allie, Julie, and Rosie cracked up.

"First stop, The Toy Chest," I announced as we cruised the mall.

"The Toy Chest?" Rosie asked. "What do we need from there?"

"Plastic spiders and any other gross things we can find," I explained.

"When I was on the beach with Kevin, the most incredibly ugly black bug jumped on my arm." Julie grimaced at the memory.

"But I bet Kevin saved you," Rosie said with a knowing look.

"Actually, we just moved to a different part of the beach." Julie pulled down the shoulder of her boatneck sweater. "Did I show you guys my tan line?"

"Only five times," Allie said.

"Does that include the three times she showed it off in biology class?" Rosie asked.

"I did not!" Julie looked worried. "Maybe my sweater slipped a little, but I wasn't trying to show off. I mean, *Mark*'s in our biology class!" Mark Harris was Julie's current heartthrob.

"What about Kevin?" Rosie asked mischievously.

Julie retorted, "He's in Florida. Mark Harris is right here in Canfield."

When Rosie shook her head, her silver earrings sparkled and her dark hair fluttered around her shoulders. I'm sure none of my friends—not even Allie—know that sometimes I practice shaking my head in front of a mirror. I'd love to do it like Rosie. But my hair is really wavy and doesn't exactly flutter. And dangly earrings that sparkle and shine just aren't my style.

We split up when we got to The Toy Chest. Allie and I went down the aisle that had all kinds of plastic creatures. Rosie and Julie took the aisle with all the sale stuff.

I grabbed a big, ugly plastic tarantula and walked it toward Allie. "Al-li-son Gra-ay, I want yooou."

"Don't!" She swatted it away.

"It's only pretend," I said, laughing. "Anyway, you can't let the kids see you're afraid of these.

Seven-year-olds will make you miserable if they think you're scared."

"I know," she moaned. When I'd turned and started looking at some rubber lizards, she grabbed a huge fake cockroach and pushed it at my face.

"Yuck!" I shoved it away from my nose.

"Scared?" she asked me.

I tried to sound cool. "Of course not. You just surprised me."

"Look at this!" Allie cried, paying no attention to my I'm-not-bothered act. She handed me a package.

"Webs?" The package didn't say much more than that. But the drawings showed filmy webs stretched across doorways and hanging from light fixtures. "Talk about setting the mood," I said.

"Gross! It's perfect."

"Let's show the others." We hurried to the sale aisle, where Rosie and Julie were trying out jump ropes.

"What are those for? Are we going to lasso monsters?" I asked.

Rosie caught her rope and hung it over the rack with the others. Julie sneaked in a few more jumps.

"There's nothing here. What did you guys find?"

In a spooky Dracula voice, I told her, "Spiders . . . und vebs." I followed with my best evil laugh.

Rosie looked through our basket. While Julie

reached past us to hang up her rope, Rosie tossed the plastic tarantula on the floor in front of her.

Julie glanced down and shrieked.

We covered our mouths and tried not to laugh too hard.

"You guys!" She leaned down and picked it up.

"Was your beach bug anything like this?" Rosie asked. Her dancing eyes said she really didn't care about the bug. She wanted to hear more about Kevin.

Knowing Rosie and Julie could talk about boys for hours, I thought I'd better take charge. "Let's buy these things and hit The Perfect Party."

"Right." Allie nearly raced me to the cash register. I guess she didn't want to hear more about Kevin either.

"Did I tell you about the zoo?" Julie asked at Perfect Party. She picked up a big pink feather and fanned herself.

"Was Kevin there?" Rosie asked, looking at paper plates. She wasn't going to let Julie forget that on her postcards to each of us she'd bragged about meeting a boy.

Julie giggled. She knew we were teasing her. "No. But Goldie wore a big green straw hat with bright feathers on it, and the birds were jealous."

"Come on. Animals can't be jealous." Allie clucked her tongue.

"Then why did the parrots turn their backs and refuse to talk for her?" Julie asked.

"Maybe they were on break," Rosie suggested.

"And the peacock," Julie continued. "He was showing off his big tail until Goldie and I got there. He saw her hat and closed his tail in shame."

"I'm sure." Did she really expect us to believe her crazy story? I was beginning to get a little annoyed with Julie.

"I guess you had to be there." Julie dropped the pink plume back into the bin and strolled down the next aisle.

"What next?" Allie asked.

Rosie started to follow Julie, wondering aloud, "How did we ever survive a week without her?"

I had a question of my own. Why was I getting so upset at Julie? Allie got better grades than me in biology and Rosie always did better in math, but I never got angry with them. And I usually enjoyed Julie's funny stories, like the one she had just told about Goldie.

I finally realized what really had been going on. I was jealous. Julie had flown off to Florida for a special week with her grandmother while I stayed in Canfield, grandparentless.

But now Julie was back with her crazy stories and

her legendary appetite, not to mention the tan line. How could anyone stay mad at her? Besides, I didn't have to be jealous anymore. I had been adopted. Maybe Miss Laura and Max weren't quite the same as real grandparents, but they made me feel pretty good.

"Anyone for cold, wet spaghetti?" I asked. We were in the kitchen at my house, and I was taking my monster dishes out of the refrigerator.

"No, thanks!" Allie said.

"I had something more like potato chips in mind," said Julie.

Rosie pushed up the sleeves of her cream-colored sweater. "I'll try. Are you going to blindfold me?"

I glanced around the kitchen. The only dish towel I saw was wet and grungy. "Just close your eyes."

"How long do I have to keep them shut?" Rosie asked.

I set the bowl on the counter and guided her hands toward the bowl. Without warning her, I shoved her hands into the slippery pasta.

"Ee-yew." Rosie frowned. "It feels like . . . like . . . worms!"

"That's great! Hey, guys, it works!" I was pleased.

Julie pushed Rosie out of the way and stretched out her hands. "Let me try."

"Close your eyes. We'll tell you what to do next," Rosie said, winking at me behind Julie's back.

When Julie scrunched her eyes shut, Rosie grabbed the bowl of peeled grapes from the top shelf in the fridge. She turned one of Julie's hands around and dropped three naked grapes into her palm. "What do these feel like?"

Julie started to open one eye.

"No peeking!" I called.

"But I don't know what you just put in my hand. It sure isn't wet spaghetti. They're round and kind of squishy." Julie was turning the grapes around in her hand, rolling them between her fingers.

Rosie couldn't help taking advantage of the fact that Julie hadn't been at Sunday's planning meeting. "Do they feel anything like . . . eyeballs?"

"Yaah!" She threw the grapes out of her hands and jumped back two feet.

Over at the table, Allie burst out laughing. "I hope seven-year-olds are as funny as you and Rosie!"

"You guys!" Julie tried to sound angry, but the big grin on her face gave her away.

"What next?" Rosie asked, looking to me for direction.

"Well, I know we talked about cottage cheese—"

"Seven-year-olds will never eat it!" Julie yelped.

Allie sighed. "They're not *going* to eat it, you nut!

They're going to stick their hands in it and think it's brains!"

"Gross!" Julie was horrified.

"It *is* gross. That's the idea," Rosie said.

"Yeah, but which one of us wants to do *that*?" Julie asked.

"That's what I was trying to say," I said. "I think the other stuff worked fine. We don't have to test the cottage cheese idea."

Julie seemed relieved, but Rosie and Allie were unconvinced.

"What if it's a flop at the party?" Rosie wanted to know.

Allie grimaced. "Okay, give me the cottage cheese. I'll try it." That idea worked, too—the look on her face was great. While Allie washed her hands, I got another bowl out of the refrigerator.

"How about the Jell-O? I'm not sure it's going to firm up with spiders in it."

Julie shivered. "I can't believe you came up with all this stuff."

"Serves you right for going away," Rosie joked.

"We made this an hour ago, so it's starting to get thick." I poked around the bowl with a wooden spoon. "Who's got the little bugs?"

"I do." Allie brought over rubber spiders and a plastic centipede. She let them fall and they hit the Jell-O with a plop.

"They're just sitting on top," Rosie said.

I pushed one down into the Jell-O with the spoon. "We could serve Jell-O squares with the bugs at the bottom. They wouldn't find them right away."

"If we put whipped topping on the squares they wouldn't see the bugs until they'd been eating for a while." Rosie raised her eyebrows and looked very devious.

"Or we could put the bugs in the whipped topping!" Julie picked up the tarantula and grinned. "Can you imagine finding this in your food?"

"Not in my restaurant," Russell said, coming into the kitchen.

"We're trying to invent gross food and games for the monster bash," Allie told him.

He strolled into the kitchen, glancing at our plastic creatures. When he saw the centipede on the top of the Jell-O bowl, he looked interested. "Is it okay if the boys want to play with the food?"

"Maybe." I wasn't sure what he had in mind.

"What if we mixed a big vat of Jell-O and filled it with your buggy friends? You could challenge the kids to dig into the slime. Each kid gets one minute to feel around. Whoever finds the most creatures wins a prize."

"I love it!" Julie exclaimed. "Can't you just see the kids with green slime up to their elbows?"

"I hope their parents won't mind if we send them home sticky," Allie worried.

"These are little boys?" Russell asked.

"Seven years old," I told him.

"No problem." He ruffled my hair. "Their parents are probably used to them coming home messy."

"Besides," Allie considered, "it'll rinse off with water. We should try to clean them up—at least a little. But you're right, Mr. Bartlett. My brother Mike used to come home messier than anything when he was seven. And you know what? He's ten now and nothing's changed. He's still a slob!"

Russell laughed. Then he checked his watch. "I've got to get to work. But I'm sure you can think of some more horrible things to do to those innocent little boys."

"Innocent?" Allie rolled her eyes. "I have two younger brothers, and I swear they've never been innocent in their lives!"

I thought about David, who'd never miss a chance to tease me. "You've got that right," I said with feeling.

Russell looked at me and raised his eyebrows. "Do I hear the voice of experience speaking?" he said. "It sounds like you'd rather put real bugs in the Jell-O." He squeezed my arm to let me know he was kidding. "See you at dinner, Beck."

"So what other terrible things can we do to the kids at the party?" Julie asked.

We reviewed the plans we'd made on Sunday so Julie could add her ideas. She had some good ones. I was glad she was back, and even happier that my bad feelings had evaporated into thin air.

"Are we done with party planning for now?" Julie asked. Before anyone replied, she was peering into the refrigerator. "Is there anything in here to eat besides worms, eyeballs, and buggy green Jell-O?"

Six

"Julie, I love your sweatshirt!" Allie said.

"I really like the sequins," Rosie added.

"Hey, you guys, I thought we were all walking home so we could discuss Saturday's party, not have a fashion show," I said.

"Really?" Allie looked confused. "I thought we were walking home because we hung around your locker so long that we missed our bus."

"Well, we could have called somebody's parents for a ride. Instead, we're having a mobile meeting," Rosie said, settling the discussion. "Julie, I bet I know where you got that sweatshirt. Goldie sent it to you."

Julie looked surprised. "How did you know?"

"Well, you've just been to visit Goldie in Florida," Rosie began. "And Goldie always mails you exotic presents. Your shirt is obviously new. And didn't you say you and Goldie had seen all those neat birds at the zoo?"

The sweatshirt had a big parrot on the front. Its eye was a black button, and sequins made its wing and tail feathers shine.

"That's absolutely amazing, Rosie," Julie said, grinning. "You're a regular Sherlock Holmes. I guess I set a good example for you." Before Julie had decided she wanted to be a major league baseball player, she had wanted to be a detective. For a while Julie had gone around observing us and writing stuff down in a notebook, occasionally saying things like "Aha!" and "Elementary, my dear Watson." Not that it had never paid off—she did once find a schoolbook I'd misplaced. (Of course, I had left it at her house.)

"Did the parrots at the zoo really turn their backs on Goldie?" Allie mused.

Julie smiled impishly. "Would I lie to you? Besides, you've probably never seen a hat like the one Goldie had on that day."

"We're halfway home," I announced. "Let's call this mobile meeting to order."

"Aye, aye, Captain Bartlett," Julie said, saluting.

I smiled and returned the salute. "Allie, is the money under control?"

"As long as we can bring the monster costume supplies from home, we'll make a profit." Allie blushed a faint pink. She was still embarrassed about having forgotten to figure in the profit on our first job. But we all knew she wouldn't make that mistake twice.

"Oh!" Julie waved her hand in the air as though we were in school. "About the monster costume contest. Could we make it a team deal?"

"I like that." We hadn't planned any team events. And we'd done enough parties to know how bored kids could get waiting for their turn at a game.

"I'll give them each a head start with face paintings," Rosie said. "Then even when they take off their costumes, they'll still look monstery when their parents pick them up."

"I had one other idea," I ventured. "You know how little kids love to make noise. What if we have a contest to see who can make the best monster sound?"

"Only if I can bring my earplugs," Allie told her.

"You really have earplugs?" Julie asked with interest.

Allie shifted her bookbag from one shoulder to the other. "Sure. How else do you think I can study with four brothers and sisters in the house?"

Julie grew thoughtful. "Maybe I should try them. Then I wouldn't have to listen to Laurel when she's on the phone with one of her boyfriends." Laurel was Julie's fifteen-year-old sister. She seemed to have a zillion boyfriends, and practically lived on the telephone.

"Has the receiver fused to her ear yet?" Rosie asked.

Julie giggled. "Not yet. But I did suggest that she think about having it surgically implanted. It would be so convenient. She could wash dishes or do homework without having to hold onto the phone."

"Speaking of homework, that reminds me," Allie said, turning toward me. "I can't study with you tonight. The whole family is going to visit Grandma."

"You'll have fun there," I told her. I hadn't seen Miss Laura and Max since the day I'd gone to Pine Villa with Allie, but I hoped to go back soon.

Allie shook her head. "Grandma can't take *all* of us down to the community room. Can you imagine Mouse running around in there?"

"Well, maybe not everyone would appreciate it," I said. "Especially not if he tries to pretend that everyone's an alien and zaps them with his ray gun, like he did when I came to your house for dinner last week. But you could still have a good time."

Allie disagreed. "It's not the same when you're not there, Becky. I don't know what to say to all those old people. It seemed so easy for you."

"They were neat people," I said. Talking to them hadn't seemed strange at all.

"I know what you mean, Allie." Julie pushed her sweatshirt sleeves up to her elbows. "When I first got to Florida, I couldn't think of much to say to Goldie."

"Not Goldie!" Rosie gave Julie a you're-kidding-me look. "She's the greatest grandmother in the world."

"Still . . ." Julie bit her lip. "Talking on the phone or visiting when she's here with the whole family isn't hard. But when I got to her house it seemed funny. It was just the two of us, and all of a sudden we seemed so different. Then somehow we started talking about guys and everything was all right."

"Wouldn't work for me," Allie grumbled. "I can't imagine discussing boys with my grandmother."

"Then I'm sure you have something else in common," Julie insisted. "Grandmothers are neat!"

I agreed with all my heart. Julie and Allie were so lucky! The people I'd met at Pine Villa were fun. I wanted Allie to get to know them better. Wouldn't it be fun if Julie and Rosie could meet them, too? Julie and Max could share Goldie stories—

Suddenly, I had an idea. We needed a party to get to know each other better! And who was better qualified to throw it than me? After all, parties are my business.

"Are you okay?" Allie asked worriedly. "You gasped like you had a pain or something."

"I'm fine," I assured her. My new idea wasn't anything I wanted to share with my friends yet. I needed some time to work on it.

"Are you *sure* you're all right?" Rosie said.

I stuck out my arm. "Check my pulse if you want, but I'm really fine."

"I bet you forgot something," Julie guessed. "If it's a schoolbook, don't worry. One of us probably has it. We'll share."

I had all my schoolbooks, so I needed another excuse.

"I just remembered I promised my mom I'd be home on time today. We have an appointment," I claimed.

"What kind of appointment? Doctor? Dentist?" Rosie seemed determined to play twenty questions.

"You didn't tell me about any appointment," Allie said suspiciously.

I'm a terrible liar. "She's taking something to one of the waitresses. You know, they're having those awful midterms at the college."

Rosie nodded, remembering our earlier conversation about the exams. "I get it. You're delivering care packages," she said.

I nodded, relieved.

"That's nice," Julie said. "I wish someone would spoil *me* during exams."

We all looked at her, but Rosie spoke first. "You get spoiled enough," she said.

"By Goldie," we all finished. Julie blushed.

I cleared my throat to get their attention. "We're almost at my house. Is everything set for Saturday?"

"I've got the games under control," Julie told me.

Rosie patted my shoulder. "I'll be there with my pens, the makeup for the monster faces, and my camera."

"And I've got all the lists ready," Allie said. "What about you? Have you made all the food arrangements?"

I laughed. "Green Jell-O, wet spaghetti, and all the rest of it."

"You know, I thought this monster bash idea was silly at first," Rosie admitted. "But I think we're going to have a lot of fun on Saturday."

"Hi, Mom!" I called on my way to my room. I hurried to the back of the house before she could ask me about my day. I was just about ready to burst with my great party idea and I wanted to think about it some more.

Did they ever have parties at Pine Villa? I figured there was a turkey dinner at Thanksgiving. And someone probably came in to carol around Christmastime. What about Valentine's Day? Or the Fourth of July? But I didn't want to wait until the next holiday to have my party.

I could just hear Allie's reaction: *A party with my grandmother and all those old people? What would we do with them?* Rosie and Julie would probably feel the same way at first. But I knew Julie would love to meet Max and hear more about her mother and Goldie. And Rosie would really enjoy listening to Miss Laura's stories about being a showgirl. The trick was to get them to Pine Villa and get them talking to people.

I flopped on my bed and buried my nose in the patchwork quilt. There had to be a way to have a fun party for everyone.

Suddenly I sat up. There *was* one way to make it happen.

I'd have to do all the work myself. I'd invite them to a mystery party, and the whole thing would be a huge surprise.

Sometimes the others tease me about bulldozing ahead when I have an idea. They're right, but I can't help it. When I had an idea as good as this one, how was I supposed to forget it?

With all the practice I'd had with The Party Line, I was certain I could figure out how to put a party together on my own.

My brain was in high gear. In my mind, I could see the invitations I'd hand to my friends next week. I'd cut them in the shape of question marks. Inside,

I would write only the date and time, and tell them to meet at my house.

They would come. I knew my friends well enough to know none of them could resist a mystery—or a surprise. Speaking of surprises, who was going to be more amazed? The residents of Pine Villa, or my friends?

Seven

"*Grr*," I growled at Julie, who had her back to me. She nearly fell off the chair she was standing on.

"Cut it out, Becky!" she shrieked.

Julie stepped off the chair in the Stevenson's family room. She'd been taping black balloons and wispy spider webs to a cord we had strung from the kitchen doorway to the fireplace mantel.

She whipped a black pen out of her pocket and threatened to draw a mustache on my lip. "Your brain must have turned to cottage cheese. I'm never going to be done with this before all the kids get here."

"I'll help you. I'm done in the kitchen." I pulled up another chair and began tacking up more decorations.

In spite of Julie's prediction, we were ready and waiting by the time the doorbell began to ring. Josh raced his mother to the front door and won.

"Happy birthday, Josh!" said a redheaded kid on the front step.

"Hi, Billy." Josh grabbed the present out of Billy's hand. He looked ready to run off somewhere and rip it open.

I reached over his shoulder and lifted the present out of his grip. Fortunately, he decided not to wrestle me for it.

"We'll take the presents for now," Rosie told Josh and Billy. "We have a special time planned for opening them later."

"Come in, Billy," Allie invited him. She led him toward the spooky family room, where she and Rosie had turned a white sheet into a ghost floating down from the ceiling.

The noise in the family room grew louder and louder as the guests gathered. Finally, everyone was there.

"Are you ready for a monster bash?" Julie called in a cheerleader voice.

"Yes!"

"I can't hear you!" she shouted.

"Yes!"

"Then let's see if you can sound like monsters," she challenged them. They took her literally. All six boys started growling and moaning. Julie waved her hands in the air. "Wait a minute!"

Josh snarled once more. Then all the boys gazed at Julie, waiting.

"This is supposed to be a contest. How can the judges tell who has the best monster voice if you all go at once?"

"Who are the judges?" Billy wanted to know.

Julie waved her hand toward the three of us. "We are."

"But you're girls," Josh pointed out.

Julie planted her hands on her hips and I got worried. Next to me, Rosie looked worried, too. We had gone through the whole girls-aren't-as-good-as-boys thing when we had to throw a party for Casey Wyatt, one of the boys in our class. But these were just *little* boys.

"You think we don't know anything about monsters?" I asked them. They shook their heads. I knew I had to do something more dramatic than plugging my fingers in my ears and sticking out my tongue.

Julie read my mind. She jumped on a chair and hunched over, keeping one shoulder higher than the other. I think she was trying to be the Elephant Man or maybe the Hunchback of Notre Dame. Anyway, she screwed up her face into a nasty expression and growled at the amazed boys. They backed off.

Julie leaped off the chair and made claws of her fingers. She jumped toward Josh.

"Hey!" he said.

"Convinced Julie knows monsters?" I asked them.
"Yeah!"

"I wish my sister could do that," Allen announced.

Julie turned back into a regular girl. "Are you ready for the contest?"

The boys nodded and lined up. Josh pushed his way to the front. "It's my birthday. I'm first."

"You each get two chances to make your best monster sounds," Julie instructed.

Josh couldn't wait for any more rules. He opened his mouth so wide I could see his tonsils and howled. He sounded kind of like a cross between a werewolf and the dog that used to live next door to my house.

Julie chuckled. "That was good. Want to do one more?"

"Sure." He grinned like a perfectly normal kid just before he wrinkled his nose and started to snort. He sounded like an angry vampire pig.

"Thank you!" Julie called loudly so Josh could hear her. Mercifully, he stopped snorting.

The other boys were just as loud, but none of them sounded as scary as Josh. It didn't seem quite right to give the first prize to the birthday boy, but each of us had voted for him.

"Josh Stevenson," Julie announced to the anxious seven-year-olds, "you have won the monster yell game."

She handed him a large rubber lizard, and he promptly shook it in her face. Julie was cool, though. She snapped at the creature, pretending to bite off its nose. The boys loved it.

"Ready for another game?" she asked the boys.

"Yeah!"

"Who will win this time?"

Each boy raised his hand. Josh tried to stretch his hand higher than the others. But Billy one-upped him. He planted one hand on poor David's back and pushed himself taller so his hand was higher than Josh's.

"Hey, guys! This isn't a contest to see who can touch the ceiling," Julie teased.

Rosie disappeared into the kitchen and came back with two big garbage bags. She winked at Julie.

As the game leader, Julie explained the monster race. "Now that you can all sound like monsters, it's time for you to dress like monsters."

The boys forgot their hand-in-the-air competition. With their eyes opened wide, they listened.

"Okay, split up into two teams." When the boys couldn't agree on who should be on whose team, Allie jumped in to help.

"David, Allen, and Zack, you're on one team," she said. "Billy, Josh, and Evan, you'll be on the other."

With the teams settled, Julie handed each group one of the large plastic trash bags. "There's enough stuff in each bag for three costumes. The team with the most disgusting monsters will win. Ready, set, go!"

The boys dug into their bags. Torn clothes, masks, hats, boots, and other monster accessories flew everywhere.

Billy tried on a wrinkly mask. It was too large for his head, but he held it in place with one of the beat-up hats Allie had found at her house.

On the other team, Josh grabbed a pair of clumsy old boots. The right boot slipped on easily, but he couldn't get his foot through the opening of the left one. Too late, he discovered the knots in the laces.

Evan had problems buttoning the "bloodstained" shirt. (It's surprising how gross dried ketchup can look.) The would-be monster couldn't get the buttons through the crusty buttonholes. When he leaned over to take a closer look, his plastic nose fell off.

Josh continued to struggle with the boots.

We'd put tape on some of Rosie's fake fingernails and painted them black. They made great claws for David's monster. Then he stuck a scar decal to his cheek and grabbed the black eye patch.

Rosie pulled out her camera and started snapping pictures. Julie bustled between the teams, making sure things stayed under control. Allie and I ducked into the kitchen to prepare the gooey green monster grope. Allie spread a plastic cloth on the kitchen floor before I set the enormous bowl in the center. We knew the game would be messy and we didn't want to leave the Stevensons' kitchen all sticky.

"Come back!" Julie called to us. "I need judges."

The four of us stood together and whispered about the boys. I had to cover my mouth to keep from laughing. None of the boys were very scary. In fact, they were all pretty cute.

Finally, Julie smiled at David's team and declared, "We have a winner!"

"Aw!" Josh thumped his boot on the floor. The laces were still hopelessly tangled.

The boys on David's team loved their prizes: eight-by-ten autographed pictures of Six-Toe, the hottest monster in Saturday morning cartoons. Allie had seen them advertised one day when she was watching cartoons with Mouse, and she'd sent away for them.

Evan shoved Josh, and we could tell they were getting tired of that game. Julie clapped her hands. "It's time to get out of the monster stuff." She needed help. Rosie set the camera on a chair and hurried to help Julie with the Billy-Josh-Evan team. Allie helped David peel the scar off his cheek while I tried to get the other boys disentangled from their costumes.

"Into the kitchen," Julie called once all the costume parts were piled on the floor.

"Is it time to eat already?" Billy asked.

"I want to play more games," Evan complained.

Once they were inside the kitchen, they stopped grumbling and stared.

"What's that?" David asked without taking his eyes off the steaming cauldron on the stove.

"And that?" Josh pointed to the plastic tablecloth in the middle of the kitchen floor.

David continued to watch the stove.

"It's monster potion," I said breezily, as if I brewed it every day.

"Wh-what's in it?" Zack wanted to know.

Rosie looked at me. "Did we use the mouse tails this time?"

The boys squinted at us. They couldn't decide whether or not to believe her.

"It's not ready yet, anyway," Julie told them. "Let's play another game in the meantime."

She got them to sit in a circle around the Jell-O bowl. Then I dumped the glop out of the bowl.

"All right!" Josh exclaimed when the jiggly green stuff plopped onto the plastic.

"You can see spiders and flies and other things in the Jell-O," Julie explained. "When I say *go*, you dig into the goo. Whoever finds the most stuff wins."

The search-and-get-sticky game was the highlight of the party. Evan's arms were green all the way to his elbows. Billy got behind in the race, because he kept licking his fingers. David kept glancing at the monster potion.

Julie wrinkled her nose delicately as she counted each boy's collection of gunky insects. As she counted, I rinsed off each bug and gave it to Rosie, who dried it. Allie, patient from years of living with brothers, gingerly washed each boy's hands and arms with a damp cloth. "Evan wins this time." She pointed to the plastic tarantula hanging from the web over the kitchen table. "After we eat, that will be yours."

"Cool!" Evan grinned and the other boys looked jealous.

"It's time for monster treats," I announced.

"Like what?" Billy wanted to know.

"Aw, it's just gonna be a cake," Josh said.

"That's what you think," Rosie told the boys as she and Julie began blindfolding them.

Josh tugged on the cloth being tied around his head. "Hey, what are you doing?"

"It's simple," Julie told him while she knotted his blindfold. "You have to guess what it is before you get to eat it."

"What kind of food is it?"

"Hmm." Julie wasn't going to give any hints. Allie got the bowl of wet spaghetti from the refrigerator. I got the plate of peeled grapes. At the last minute we'd decided against the cottage cheese.

None of us—not even Allie—wanted to have to wash the boys' hands again. And we were pretty sure they wouldn't want us to. We set the dishes on the counter and let the boys approach them one at a time. Rosie sneaked off to a corner to work on the real treats.

Allen plunged his hands into the cold spaghetti. He made a face when he realized his hands weren't touching cake frosting. "Gross! What is it?"

"That's for you to tell us."

He thought for half a minute before he announced, "My sister's hair." (That made me very curious about Allen's sister.)

Next, Julie led Josh to the grape plate. He brushed his hands over the fruit and shivered. But he acted brave and said, "His sister's hair? Allen's crazy. These are toads." With his blindfold still tied, he let Julie lead him back to his friends. He shook his head and told the other boys, "Can you believe those girls caught a bunch of toads and brought them into my house?"

"Toads?" Billy shook his head.

To make things more confusing, Julie took Evan to the spaghetti bowl. When his fingers touched the wet noodles, I saw him wrinkle his nose beneath his blindfold. Then he asked, "We're gonna eat worms?"

"Worms?" Josh clearly thought his friend was crazy.

"Yeah. Worms." Evan was not concerned by Josh's tone of voice. "They feel just like the worms my Uncle Todd digs before he takes me fishing, except these are all smooth instead of dirty."

David made a gagging sound. "We're eating worms and toads?"

Julie bit her lip to keep from giggling. After the other boys had their turns, she nodded to Allie and me. We scurried to get the chocolate cake out of hiding. I peeked over Rosie's shoulder and saw that she was painting chocolate sauce webs over scoops of ice cream.

"You've all been good sports," Julie told the boys. "But we wouldn't make you eat worms and toads. Take off your blindfolds and see what monsters like for dinner."

Josh was the first to slip his blindfold over his head and toss it to the floor. His eyes narrowed in disbelief when he saw the plate. "Grapes? I thought they were toads!"

Evan and Allen both laughed when they saw the spaghetti. "It could have been worms," Evan told his friend. "But you said it felt like your sister's hair."

"Well, she puts all kinds of junk on it," Allen said to defend himself.

Allie brought the cake to the kitchen counter. "Happy birthday to you," we all sang.

"I told you it was gonna be chocolate cake," Josh said proudly as the first piece was cut.

"Can I have the wart on the monster's chin?" Billy asked, nearly sticking his finger into the frosting face.

"Wait for the ice cream." Rosie was balancing three bowls on her arm.

"Cool!" the boys cried when they saw the webs she'd drawn over the top of their vanilla ice cream. She had even trapped some chocolate insects.

"This is a great party!" Billy told Josh.

David didn't say anything. He kept glancing from his empty cup to the pot on the stove.

"I almost forgot the drinks!" I cried. David's face looked like he couldn't decide if he was excited or terrified.

Allie helped me lift the pitcher out of the pot and the dry ice, hoping the boys couldn't see what we were doing. To make it more convincing, I used an oven mitt when I carried the pitcher to the table, pretending the potion was boiling hot. The boys were quiet as I filled their paper cups with dark liquid.

The birthday boy wasn't about to wait for someone else to be brave. He took a tiny sip. "Aw! It's just grape juice. I knew my mom wouldn't let you poison us."

The boys snickered. No one would admit they had been worried.

"Hey!" Josh yelled. "What about my presents?"

The rest of the party sped along, from Josh's presents to monster face painting by Rosie and more games by Julie. What was I doing all that time? Mostly trying to rescue all the reusable party supplies that I could, so I could use them for the Pine Villa party. The second the boys finished their ice cream, I grabbed their plastic dishes and rinsed them in the kitchen sink. I wiped off the plastic tablecloth and tucked it away in one of my bags.

"What are you? A pack rat?" Allie asked. I hadn't seen her come into the kitchen.

"Just trying to clean up," I said, hoping to sound innocent. She shrugged and left. I went back to work. There were some candies on the kitchen counter, leftovers from making the goodie bags. I scooped them up and zipped them into a sandwich bag.

"Becky!" Allie called from the front room. "The kids are leaving."

I tucked all my salvaged supplies away in a grocery bag. "I'll be right there."

Evan's mom was listening intently as her son raved about the party. As he talked about monster potion and worms and toads, she looked slightly bewildered. She laughed when he waved the plastic tarantula in her face.

"I'm glad he had such a great time," she told us.

"It was awesome!" Evan said.

"Do you have a business card?" she asked. "My daughter has a birthday coming up soon."

I pulled a Party Line flyer out of my pocket and handed it to her. She smiled at our logo, which is a telephone with a long cord that spells out our company name.

When all the boys were gone, we collapsed in the kitchen. Julie snuck a piece of cake. Allie took out the party garbage.

Rosie stood on a chair in the family room and started to peel the spider web from the ceiling. "Think we'll get a job from Evan's mom?"

"You never know," I told her. We get a lot of new business from parents whose children come to our parties.

"Just as long as it's not another monster party," Julie said with a sigh. "I'm going to see spiders and bugs in my dreams."

"That will teach you not to take any more vacations," Rosie told her.

"Really," Allie added. "If you're gone when Evan's mom calls, we just might do this all over again!"

Eight

"I'm glad everyone is here," I said when Julie got on the school bus Monday morning.

"Why is Becky grinning like a fool? Did her mom win the lottery or something?" Julie asked Rosie. Rosie shrugged her shoulders.

Rosie and Julie peered at Allie. After all, she was my very best friend. If anyone knew why I was so happy, it would be Allie. But I hadn't told her anything about my plan. It nearly killed me to keep quiet, but I had to.

"Is there something you want to tell us?" Allie finally asked. "Did The Party Line get a new job?"

"Not a job," I told them. "But you've got the party part right. I'm inviting each of you to a party on Thursday."

All I got were three very puzzled looks. I handed them the invitations. Cutting them in the shape of question marks had worked out great. Since I wasn't telling them everything, it seemed appropriate.

Julie waved her invitation in the air. "What kind of party is this?"

"A mystery party?" Allie guessed, trying to figure out the theme.

"Yeah." Leave it to Allie to figure it out. We've been friends so long we can sometimes finish each other's sentences. "It's a mystery."

"That's why it just says to meet at your house after school on Thursday." Rosie smiled. I could tell the puzzle appealed to her. She couldn't resist asking, "Who else will be there?"

"Will there be any boys there?" Julie wanted to know.

"Maybe." It wasn't exactly a lie. Okay, so the boys at Pine Villa all had gray hair—or no hair at all—but technically they were boys.

"What do we need to do? Or bring?" Organized Allie was asking her typical questions. "Should I be filling out a form?"

I laughed. "It's a personal party, not a job. No forms. But I *could* use a little help."

Julie sat up. "What can we do?"

"If you have any extra party supplies, bring them with you on Thursday."

"That sounds easy enough. I could bring my glitter gun, too," Rosie volunteered.

"That would be great." The party was beginning to look easy if all my friends were going to help.

"And bring your camera," Allie told Rosie. "This party sounds like we might need pictures."

"Right."

"This is important," Ms. Pernell told us during sixth period biology, pointing to the chalkboard.

I knew I should copy the chart she had written up there, but I was too busy. Since I wanted to have cookies at the Pine Villa party instead of cake, I had to figure out how many batches to bake. And I'd have to see if the retirement complex had a punch bowl I could borrow.

Pine Villa! I'd forgotten to call Ms. Hawkins, the social director, last Friday to confirm the party time. What if they had something else scheduled for then? I *had* to call her the second I got home from school.

I used my red pen to write a reminder across the top of my notes: *"Call Ms. Hawkins."*

Allie tried to peek at my notes. I quickly opened my science book so it blocked her view. My friend wrinkled her nose at me and tapped Julie on the shoulder.

When Julie turned her head, Allie nodded in my direction. Julie stretched tall and glanced over her shoulder.

I casually covered the red message to myself with my hand, and pretended to be very interested in Ms. Pernell's lecture. My strategy worked. After a couple of puzzled looks at me, they both lost interest and looked back at the chalkboard. Well, maybe it didn't have much to do with my attitude. We were having a test on Friday, and my friends had more important things to think about than what I'd written at the top of my notes.

I went back to my private project. If I planned to bake cookies and mix punch, I'd need ingredients. I tried to start a list but soon realized it was impossible without looking at my mom's recipes.

Even if I used her recipes, though, I wasn't going to ask her to help. The Pine Villa party was my own special project. I'd make all the food myself, and I'd pay for all the ingredients and everything else I'd need. Between my job at the Moondance and my share of The Party Line's profits, I had saved enough money to put on my party.

I thought of Miss Laura and Max. And I smiled.

"What's so funny?" Allie whispered from the desk next to mine.

"I'm just happy," I replied softly.

"Have you got a question about this chart, Becky?" Ms. Pernell inquired.

I shook my head.

"Allie?" Ms. Pernell asked.

Allie shook her head. Allie rarely had to ask any questions. She took such great notes that she never had any problems.

I had lots of questions, of course, but I couldn't ask them. I didn't want Ms. Pernell to know I hadn't been paying attention. I figured I'd ask Allie to go over it with me before Friday's test.

The bell rang. Ms. Pernell watched the four of us as we walked out the door and headed for social studies.

"What's with her today?" Rosie asked.

"She probably wanted to know about Becky's secret notes," Julie said.

"What secret notes?" Rosie sat in front of me and hadn't seen what was going on.

Allie sighed and cocked her head toward me. "Ask *her*."

Rosie stared at me with her big green eyes. I took a deep breath and bit my tongue. They weren't going to get the story out of me. The party was going to be a surprise.

Instead of discussing the party, I asked all of them, "Who wants to loan me their biology notes from today?"

Allie rolled her eyes toward the ceiling. "You were writing enough to be taking notes for *all* of us!"

"If you weren't copying the chart, what *were* you doing?" Julie wanted to know.

I smiled mysteriously and told them, "Something more important."

"More important than one of Pernell's bio tests?"

Rosie stopped and stared at me in complete amazement. Biology wasn't my best class, and my friends knew it. But the Pine Villa party was even bigger than Friday's test. I kept walking, and Rosie hurried to catch up to us.

When no one offered to help me study for the test, I had to ask, "Does this mean no one wants to share their notes?"

Allie patted me on the shoulder. "Of course not. I think Ms. Pernell finally got to you and you lost it last period. I can take pity on a crazy person."

I opened my mouth to tell her I wasn't crazy, but I realized that would just make my friends ask more questions. Instead, I grinned. They could think whatever they wanted.

"Why don't you come over to my house when we get back from Winter's?" Allie said.

"Winter's?" I couldn't imagine what the big department store at the mall had to do with biology notes.

"She's forgotten!" Rosie said with a mock horrified gasp.

Julie reached out and touched my forehead. "She doesn't feel feverish."

"Try her pulse," Rosie suggested.

Allie grabbed my wrist and made a big show of pretending to take my pulse—checking her watch and counting. The others continued to talk.

"What did you have for lunch?"

"Do you feel faint?"

Rosie leaned close to my face. "When did you first notice this memory problem?"

I had no idea why they were behaving like we were in a bad soap opera. I shook Allie's hand off my wrist and bent backward to escape Rosie. "Knock it off, guys. What's the deal with Winter's?"

"The Jamboree Sale," Julie told me. When I still didn't share their excitement, she tried to spell out the news for me. "The big S-A-L-E. You know, when all the great clothes cost less than they do on regular days."

"I know what a sale is." Just then it came back to me. Rosie's mom was giving us a ride to the Pine Tree Mall for an afternoon shopping attack. "I can't go."

My friends threw up their hands. (The Jamboree really is a great sale.) "I'm really sorry, guys. There's something I have to do right after school."

"Do you absolutely, positively have to do it right then?" Rosie asked.

I nodded. I really couldn't wait any longer to call Ms. Hawkins about the party arrangements. It should have been done days ago.

"Something more important than Winter's Jamboree Sale?" Julie inquired. Plainly, she found this hard to believe.

" 'Fraid so," I said. Then I held the back of my hand to my brow, sighed, and said in my best tragic-actress voice, "I guess you'll just have to ..." I paused and gave a loud pretend sniffle. ". . . do your best without me." I was joking, but inside I felt more than a twinge of regret. The party *was* more important, but I'd really been looking forward to buying some new stuff. The Jamboree was the biggest sale of the year. Then I thought about Miss Laura and Max and Allie's grandmother. I imagined them smiling when they walked into the community room and discovered a party.

I could buy a great new outfit. Or I could do something nice for my best friends and for people I wished were my very own grandparents. Which was *really* more important? I sighed again, a real sigh. *Oh well*, I thought, *there's always next year's Jamboree.*

Nine

"We're here!" Julie screamed. It was Thursday afternoon.

All three of them burst through the door. At least, it seemed like they all tried to squeeze into the kitchen at the same time. And they might have succeeded if they hadn't all been carrying bags and boxes of party supplies.

Rosie stumbled into the kitchen first. She looked in the big bag on the counter, the one with all the punch ingredients. "Hey. It *is* a party!"

"You bet." I said. "A party to go."

"What do you mean, party to go?" Allie asked. "Why can't we have it here?"

Julie, meanwhile, was looking around. "I think I know why we're not having it here." There were cookie crumbs on the floor and water puddles on the counter. Okay, so I had dropped a couple of cookies when I tried to slide them into the shoeboxes and, well, I hadn't found time to wipe up the spots where

I'd been defrosting the frozen juices. But I'd neatly piled the apple cores and orange pits off to one side, at least. The cleaning would have to wait. We were expected at Pine Villa in less than half an hour.

"Uh, Becky," Allie said, staring at the mess, "is this going to be a Clean-the-Bartletts'-House party?"

"No." I stacked one cookie-filled shoebox on top of the other and put them into a large carton. "The party is somewhere else. And it's time for us to get going."

While I was talking, Rosie, perfectionist that she is, had found a dish towel and dried the puddles on the counter. "I wish I could sweep the floor, too," she said. "Your mom won't be too happy to see it. But if Madame President says we leave, we leave."

The problem with my big carton was that I had to hold it even or else the cookies slid around inside. I didn't want them crumbling to pieces before I even got out of the house! To protect them, I had to hold the carton with both hands. But that didn't leave me a hand to grab the grocery bag.

"Need some help?" Rosie asked. She balanced her own bag on one hip and then reached for mine.

"Thanks."

"No problem." She peered into the open bag. "And now I know something about the party that no one else knows, except Becky."

"What?" The others craned their necks, but Rosie protected my bag.

She raised her eyebrows as if she knew a national secret. Then she laughed and said, "We're going to have Becky's famous tutti-frutti punch."

"Let's *go*!" I called.

Rosie and I were the first to leave the house. We were halfway down the wood steps when Julie and Allie closed the door behind them.

"And now—" Julie paused for effect and I could hear the smile in her voice. "Let's party!"

Rosie started humming the tune of Vermilion's newest single. Allie snapped her fingers to keep the beat.

We were on the sidewalk when all four of us began to sing, "Gonna have a good time, oh yeah. Party, and good friends, and lots of fun . . ."

I didn't know all the verses, so I had to start humming about halfway through the song. But Allie knew all the words. Vermilion was her favorite singer in the whole world.

It was nice to see Allie singing so unselfconsciously. Before she met Vermilion at the concert she gave in Canfield a while ago, Allie would rather have eaten worms than sing in public. She had never had any trouble singing at the parties we gave, though, probably because the audiences were always just little kids and us. She had a really great voice, and meeting Vermilion—who had once been shy, too—had given Allie the courage to join glee club. I was glad she was finally letting more people hear her sing.

Allie was so busy singing she didn't realize we were on the way to Pine Villa until we were almost there. When the song was finished, she looked around. "Hey, we're near my grandma's place."

I tried to look innocent, but Allie could tell when I was hiding something. She studied my face for a minute or two before she said, "Tell me we're not going to Pine Villa."

"Pine Villa. Is that where your grandmother lives?" Rosie asked.

"Is it her birthday?" Julie looked as though she thought it was a good idea to throw a birthday party for Allie's grandmother.

"I don't think so." Allie squinted as she tried to remember her grandmother's birth date.

Julie giggled. "Don't worry, Allie. I don't know Goldie's birthday either. She refuses to have birthdays, she says, so she doesn't have to think about how old she is."

"But anyway, how would Becky know when *my* grandmother's birthday is?" Before Allie's brain overloaded trying to figure out that one, I admitted that it wasn't her grandmother's birthday.

"It's not?" Allie still sounded confused. "Then the party is for Miss Laura? Or Max?"

"Sort of." I didn't want to tell them the whole story until we were inside the community room. *Maybe I can talk Ms. Hawkins into locking the door so they can't escape,* I thought worriedly.

"Ooh, I know! They're getting married!" Rosie exclaimed. Leave it to Rosie to see a romantic angle in everything. She sighed and, true to form, said, "How wonderful!"

"Rosie, Max and Miss Laura are not getting married, OK?" When I saw the disappointment on her face, I added, "Sorry."

Ms. Hawkins met us in the front lobby. "Hi, girls. I've been waiting for you."

I checked my watch. We were about five minutes late. "Can we go right to the community room and start decorating?"

"Follow me." Ms. Hawkins hurried through the lobby with us behind her. Julie and Rosie were curious. They looked around as if they were on an adventure. Allie kept giving me strange looks.

"Where is everybody?" Julie asked. "Are they all taking naps?"

"Julie!" Rosie sounded appalled at the suggestion that old people needed naps.

Julie smiled. "Hey, Goldie believes in siestas."

"Some of our residents do rest after lunch, but

right now they're all outside on the lawn," Ms. Hawkins explained. "I didn't want anyone to wander into the community room before everything was ready."

"That would ruin our surprise." I appreciated all of her help. Ms. Hawkins was really taking the party seriously, and that made me feel good. "Thanks."

I was surprised when she opened the double doors to our party room. One whole wall was windows that let in the afternoon light. I hadn't noticed that on my other visit.

Ms. Hawkins walked to one end of the windows and reached for a drapery cord. "Do you want the curtains open or closed?"

Aha! The drapes had been closed during my Monday night visit. "I think it's nice with the curtains open."

"But what about the, uh, residents?" Allie asked, following Ms. Hawkins's lead and not calling the Pine Villa seniors "old people." "Will the light bother them?"

Ms. Hawkins smiled. Rosie was not so polite. "What do you think they are, Allie? Vampires? They're out sitting in the sun right now."

Allie looked embarrassed. Julie patted her on the shoulder.

"Do you girls need any help from me?" Ms. Hawkins asked.

I set my carton on the table where I'd seen people playing cards. "I think we can take it from here."

"All right," Ms. Hawkins said. "I'll bring everyone in at four-fifteen. Want to synchronize watches?"

"Sure." Rosie studied her hot pink glow-in-the-dark watch. "I've got three-fifty-five."

"Me, too." Ms. Hawkins left the room and closed the doors behind her.

"We only have twenty minutes. What are we going to do?" Allie asked, panic in her voice.

I set the grocery bag with the punch supplies next to Pine Villa's punch bowl. Then I lifted the two shoeboxes out of my carton.

"Allie, you're in charge of refreshments. Mix the punch—the directions are in the bag. You'll find the fruit slices in a plastic bag in the bottom. And put the cookies on the plates you'll find at the bottom of the carton."

I turned around to tell the others I would need their help with decorations. Julie and Rosie were whispering. "What's going on?" I asked.

"Uh . . ." Julie twisted a strand of her hair. "We didn't know this was going to be a grown-up party, and the supplies we brought are kind of stupid."

"Like what?"

They both began to pull things out of their bags. There were some pointed pink party hats with grinning monkeys printed on them, noisemakers, and clown napkins.

Oh, no, I thought, groaning inside. *The Pine Villa residents are going to think we're absolute idiots.* I went over and looked in the bag. Rosie did have a nice paper flower centerpiece, and I had the tablecloth that I'd rescued from the monster bash—luckily we hadn't extended the monster theme to the tablecloth. Maybe they wouldn't look too closely at the napkins. And we didn't have to use the hats.

Allie had just lifted the tablecloth out of the box. I took it from her and handed it to Rosie. "Could you set up the refreshment table with this tablecloth and your centerpiece?"

She snapped her fingers and beamed. "I'll make it special."

I knew she would. If anyone could make our supplies look like something more than leftovers, Rosie could.

"What about me, boss?" Julie asked me.

"We're going to give this room a party mood," I told her. Together we checked all the supply bags and boxes. The best thing we found was brightly colored crepe paper.

"Let's hang streamers," Julie suggested. She climbed onto a chair before I could even reply. "Hand me some tape and the red roll."

We draped the red, white, and pink streamers

from each corner of the room to the center. It looked great except for the spot in the middle of the ceiling where all the ends met. Julie and I stood under it, making faces.

"What's wrong?" Rosie asked, checking her watch. "Eight minutes to go."

I pointed to the spot over our heads. "This looks messy."

Rosie analyzed the situation. "It looks like the place where all the ribbons come together when you wrap a package."

"The spot I cover with a stick-on bow," Julie said with a laugh.

"Hmm. That just might work." Rosie's artistic vibes were taking over. In seconds, she was tying together crepe paper from all three rolls. Two minutes later, she ripped the strands from their rolls and held up a huge paper flower.

Rosie climbed on a chair and stood on her toes. Julie held the chair steady. Since they had things under control, I hurried over to Allie. "How's it going?"

She set the cookie plates on the table. "All ready."

I was pleasantly surprised. The table really looked great. The glass bowl, filled with tutti-frutti punch, sat at one end of the table. The plates of cookies were at the opposite end. In the center, Rosie had given the centerpiece a shimmer with her indispensable glitter gun.

"They're going to be here any second," Allie warned as she checked her watch.

I glanced around the room and saw the babyish party hats and noisemakers scattered on a side table. "Let's just throw this junk in a box and hide it."

Together we stuffed it all into the empty carton and stuck it behind a chair in the corner. Just as we shifted the chair to hide our box, we heard a knock.

The door opened a crack and Ms. Hawkins peeked inside. "Are you ready?"

Ten

"What's all this?" the first woman asked when she came into the room, leaning on her cane. She was smiling.

"It reminds me of my senior prom," another woman said with a sigh. "It looks like a fairyland in here."

"Look at that!" Her friend pointed to Rosie's streamer flower in the center of the ceiling. "Isn't that clever?"

Most of the other residents didn't spend much time admiring the decorations, heading straight for the refreshment table instead.

"Allie? Is that you?" Mrs. Laporte broke away from her new friends to give her granddaughter a hug and a kiss.

Suddenly, there was a lump in my throat. Mrs. Laporte was really pleased to see Allie. If I had a grandmother, I'd be the one getting hugged and kissed.

I jumped when someone tapped me on the shoulder.

"It's just me," Max said at my side.

Without taking time to think about it and get embarrassed, I took his hand and squeezed it. "*Just* you? I'm *glad* it's you."

He smiled and hugged my shoulder. "Did you do all this?"

I pointed to the streamers overhead. "My friend Rosie made the beautiful flower. And my friend Julie did the streamers."

"Don't let Becky's modesty fool you," Rosie spoke up from behind us. "This whole thing was her idea. She baked all the cookies, and it's her special tutti-frutti punch recipe. She even brought all the decorations. And she kept the whole thing a secret!"

"Well," said Max. He looked me straight in the eye. "I'm impressed. I guess I'm pretty lucky to have an adopted granddaughter like you."

Rosie looked from me to Max. "What?"

Suddenly I didn't feel so shy about talking about it anymore. "I don't have any real grandparents, but when I came here with Allie, Miss Laura and Max kind of adopted me. I think I'm the lucky one, though. I've always wanted grandparents, and now I've got a really great set."

"This is wonderful!" Miss Laura rushed toward

me and pulled me into a bear hug. I had no idea someone so old could be so strong.

"I told you she was something else—a regular pip," Max told Miss Laura.

"Of course she is. She's my adopted granddaughter. Takes after me." Miss Laura fondly tucked my hair behind my ear. Today she was dressed in a flowing purple outfit with a golden scarf trailing elegantly off one shoulder. She was wearing a long golden necklace with a huge blue jewel on it and a whole slew of bangle bracelets. She looked terrific. I could see Rosie taking in Miss Laura's outfit. She was probably making notes to herself to try trailing scarves.

"Your friend is bedazzled," Max observed.

I touched Rosie's shoulder. "Rosie, this is Max." Rosie smiled shyly and stuck out her hand. "Miss Laura," I said next, "this is my friend Rosie."

Miss Laura looked at Rosie's heart-shaped face and long, wavy black hair. "I used to have jet black hair myself, Rosie. Do you sing, by any chance?"

"Not really. But my friend Allie has an excellent voice." Rosie pointed to where Allie stood near her grandmother.

"Rosie's an artist," I said.

"Art?" Max asked. "What kind of art?"

I pointed toward the glittering centerpiece. "She decorated that."

"It must have taken hours," said a woman who had come up beside us. "Are those sparkles sequins you sewed on?"

Rosie laughed. We both knew she didn't have that much patience. "I didn't sew them on. I used my glitter gun."

"Your what?" Miss Laura inquired.

"It's like a gun, but when I pull the trigger glitter and glue come out."

Miss Laura's eyes lit up. "Oh, I'd love one of those!"

"That's all *you* need," Max said to her. He looked at Rosie. "Don't you go putting even more ideas in Miss Laura's head. It's bad enough she dresses up like a Christmas tree every day. Next you'll have her putting sparkles all over the place." He sounded exasperated, but his big grin gave him away.

Miss Laura pretended to look down her nose at Max. Then she blew it by socking him on the arm and saying, "Max, you old fool. If there weren't ladies present, I'd give you a piece of my mind. Besides, this place could use a little perking up."

Rosie and I just gaped. I don't know why, but we were both a little surprised to hear two old people kidding around just like we all do.

Julie was dragging a man toward us. She introduced me by saying, "This is the person who baked the cookies."

He took my hand in his. "Thank you. These cookies are delicious."

"Of course they are." Miss Laura said proudly. "My Becky made them."

Then she turned to me. "They really are wonderful. But I wonder, why did you ask me if *I'd* bake you cookies when you're such a good baker yourself?"

I blushed. "I don't know. I guess it just seemed like a grandmotherly thing to do. Isn't it sort of traditional—you visit your grandmother and she serves you home-baked cookies?" Now that I thought about it, I felt a little silly.

"Well, I'm hardly a traditional grandmother," Miss Laura said as she swung her long gold necklace and stood with one hand on her hip. "Do you want to trade me in?"

I was shocked. One of the things I loved about Miss Laura was that she was so . . . so original. Without thinking, I threw my arms around her.

"No, never!" I practically shouted. "You're the best."

"Okay, okay," Miss Laura grumbled. "I was just checking." Then she winked and ruffled my hair.

I noticed Max studying Julie. Was it possible she reminded him of her mother or Goldie? I had to introduce them. "Julie, this is Max. He used to be a teacher at the high school. He remembers your mother, and Goldie, too."

Julie grinned and linked her arm through his. "So you're the one who has been telling my friends about my grandmother. Isn't she great? When Goldie called last night, I got a chance to ask her about you. She said you were her favorite dance partner. . . ."

I couldn't hear any more of the conversation. Julie and Max headed for some chairs, talking nonstop. I couldn't have wished for anything better. Julie and Max were having fun. Allie was getting her grandmother a cup of punch and looked like she was having a good time, too. Miss Laura had cornered Rosie and seemed to be trying to talk her into something.

Suddenly I realized I was thirsty—very thirsty. I headed for the punch bowl.

A kind-looking man with a white beard poured a cup and handed it to me. "You must be one of the girls who are throwing this party. I'm Ted Van Doren."

"Yes, I am." I took a sip of punch. "I'm Becky Bartlett."

His gray eyes settled on my face. I felt a little strange until he spoke again. "Could I ask you something?"

"Sure."

He cleared his throat. "Why? Why are you girls doing this for us?"

I was embarrassed. How was I supposed to explain without sounding like some kind of goody-goody? I thought about how much I wanted grandparents, how much I liked Allie's grandma, Miss Laura, and Max, and how I'd wanted my three best friends to get to know my new friends. The whole time, Ted waited patiently for an answer. Finally I figured out the best way to explain it all.

"I just thought it would be fun," I told him.

"Fun? I thought girls your age spent your time shopping and chasing boys." He smiled.

"I definitely like to shop," I said, thinking about the Jamboree Sale.

"How about boys?" he said with a twinkle in his eye.

"Well . . ."

The first piano notes caught everyone's attention. Across the room, Rosie was seated on the piano bench. Miss Laura stood next to the piano, leaning her elbows on the top of it.

Miss Laura started singing. She really did have a good voice. It was low and kind of smoky-sounding. She was singing a bouncy song I recognized from Russell's record collection.

"You say poe-tay-toe, I say poe-tah-toe, you say toe-may-toe, I say toe-mah-toe. Poe-tay-toe, poe-tah-toe, toe-may-toe, toe-mah-toe—let's call the whole thing off!"

A few people around me were humming or singing softly to themselves. One old lady was just swinging her hips to the music, like a shimmy dancer.

Julie and Allie joined me at the punch table. "Do you believe it?" Julie asked.

"I just hope Miss Laura controls herself," I told them. "She used to be a showgirl."

Allie giggled. "You mean she might start dancing?"

It *was* a little hard to believe this was a retirement complex. People were tapping their feet and nodding in time to the music. It was a pretty lively crowd.

When the song ended, Miss Laura turned the page in the old music book. Rosie took a little time to experiment with the unfamiliar tune and then started to play.

Miss Laura had a mischievous smile on her face and she began rocking a little from side to side as she sang, "My mama warned me about boys like you. . . ."

Suddenly Max appeared, holding his hands out for Julie. "I'm sure Goldie's granddaughter knows how to dance. May I have this dance?"

She giggled and let him pull her away from the table.

Max was quite a dancer! So was Julie! They were

whirling around the dance floor like two pros. I could see Julie laughing as they swung around.

Everyone seemed to like Max's idea. Soon there were lots of couples bobbing around the room. No one seemed to notice when Rosie hit the occasional wrong note.

"Shouldn't we be doing something?" Allie asked me.

"Like what?"

Allie shrugged. "I don't know. But Rosie and Julie are doing all the work. I feel guilty."

Good old Allie. She worries too much. "Just have fun," I told her. "That's what everyone else is doing—even Rosie and Julie."

When the song was over, Miss Laura chose another page in the music book and started to sing again. Most of the couples stayed on the dance floor, and some new couples joined them. Max pretended to wipe his brow as he walked back with Julie. "Whew," he said. "She's Goldie's granddaughter, all right."

Julie looked a little whirled-out herself. Her eyes were bright and her cheeks were pink.

But I could hardly keep my eyes off Miss Laura. She was amazing. I listened to her for a while until, out of the corner of my eye, I saw Max. He was sitting in the corner chair, and was trying to move it forward so he could get a better view of Miss Laura.

The back leg was stuck on our hidden supply box, though.

I grabbed Allie's sleeve. "He's going to find our stuff."

"Who? What?"

My stomach sank as I watched Max peer behind the chair and lift our supplies out of their hiding place. I thought the party was about to be ruined. But he pulled out a pink party hat and smiled.

"Hey, look what I've found!" he called, forgetting Miss Laura had not finished her number.

He put the hat on his head, but the child-size elastic wouldn't stretch under his chin. Without the strap, the hat wouldn't balance atop his gray hair. So he held it with one hand and used his free hand to toss hats and noisemakers to his friends.

Miss Laura was only mad for half a minute. As soon as someone threw her a noisemaker, she put it to her lips.

"This is just like New Year's Eve!" Mrs. Laporte yelled to us.

Allie turned to me with her blue eyes opened wide. "My grandmother is screaming and wearing a pink party hat with smiling monkeys on it!"

"I think it's wonderful," Julie said with her usual enthusiasm. "This was a *great* idea, Becky."

"I second the motion." Rosie rested her hand on my shoulder.

"You know what the best part is?" Allie asked.

"The food?" Julie guessed.

"The music and the dancing?" I ventured.

Allie shook her head. "When we first got here, I thought the idea was stupid. Even if the seniors had fun, I thought I'd be bored." She gave me an apologetic look. "But I was wrong. I'm having as much fun as anyone else in this room!" That was exactly what I had wanted to happen at the party, but I'd been afraid to hope for it.

The next thing I knew, Miss Laura had started another song—and I was headed for the dance floor with Max.

Eleven

After dinner, I crashed on the family room couch with my biology notes. I tried to study. I really did.

Allie had explained the comparisons between the various species on Ms. Pernell's chart. And I had read all of the materials for the test the next day. But I kept thinking about the party.

My head was full of pictures: me dancing with Max, Max dancing with Julie, the man who loved my cookies, Miss Laura and Rosie at the piano. I closed my eyes and sighed.

"Tired?" my mom asked.

I opened my eyes quickly. I hadn't heard her sneaking up on me. Tired? I was more happy than exhausted. I told my mother, "Not really."

"You've been busy lately, but I'm not sure what you've been doing. The kitchen was a disaster area this afternoon."

Uh-oh. I hadn't gotten home until dinner time, and

I'd forgotten about the cookie crumbs on the floor. "I meant to clean up the mess. I'm sorry."

I didn't expect my mom to accept my excuse. She's really a great mom, but at our house everyone is supposed to clean up after herself or himself. When she strolled over to the couch and looked down at me, I thought I was in deep, deep trouble, and probably was going to get garbage duty for the next month.

To my utter amazement, she smiled and said, "It's okay." Then she sat on the edge of the cushion. "Tell me what was so important today."

"You really want to know?" Now that the surprise was over, it wouldn't hurt to tell her.

"You were almost glowing at dinner tonight, and it wasn't because of the meatloaf. What's up?"

I sat up and tossed my biology notes to the floor. "We had so much fun today at Pine Villa."

My mom squinted at me. "The retirement home?"

"Yeah. Allie's grandma is there. I went with Allie to visit her, and then I had this super idea to have a party for everyone."

"For everyone at Pine Villa?"

"Yes. And it was so much fun! Miss Laura was singing with Rosie. And I danced with Max. He used to know Goldie and Julie's mom—"

"Max who? And who's Miss Laura?"

"Max and Miss Laura are my adopted Pine Villa grandparents."

My mother looked totally confused. She held up her hand. "Wait. Let's back up. What kind of party was it? Was it someone's birthday?"

She sounded like Allie and the others. "Why did there have to be a reason?" I said.

"There's always a reason for a party," my mother told me. "Even if it's just to have a good time."

I supposed she was right. There are last-day-of-school parties, Valentine parties, anniversary parties, and parties for lots of other occasions. "It was a party to make the people at Pine Villa happy."

My mother bit her lower lip the way she always did when she couldn't quite understand something. Slowly, she said, "That's a wonderful thing to do, sweetie, but how did you ever get such an idea?"

I leaned back against the cushion and remembered how the idea had just popped into my head. "I guess it started when I had so much fun at Pine Villa that I wanted Julie and Rosie to meet my new friends. And Allie seemed a little uncomfortable spending time with her grandmother, so I just wanted to make it a little easier for her."

My mother nodded her head. "I guess you couldn't just take Rosie and Julie over to the retirement complex and introduce them to your new friends."

"No." (Frankly, that idea had never occurred to me.) "I wanted everyone to have fun. And they did."

"So you and your friends planned a party." My mom nodded.

"They didn't help me. I did all the work myself."

"That doesn't make any sense. Wasn't it a Party Line party?"

"They were all my guests, including Allie, Rosie, and Julie. I wanted to surprise everybody."

My mom tapped on my head. I expected to hear her usual line, which is "Is anyone in there?" Instead, she asked, "Where *do* you get your ideas, Becky?"

I told her the truth. "They just come to me."

"They still have to come from somewhere." My mother was doing her detective act. "When did you get interested in Pine Villa?"

"When Julie went to visit Goldie."

My mom blinked. It wasn't the answer she had expected. I could see she was getting confused again, so I just decided to tell her the whole story.

"I started thinking how nice it would be to have a grandmother when Julie went to see Goldie in Florida. Then Allie's grandma moved to Canfield and I went with Allie to visit her. The people there were so neat! Miss Laura even adopted me."

"Right. The adopted grandparents. I meant to get

to that." My mother rubbed her temples. I hoped I wasn't giving her a headache.

"Yeah, well, it makes sense, Mom. I wished I had a grandmother like Allie and Julie do. And when Miss Laura found out I didn't have any grandparents at all, she adopted me. She doesn't have any grandchildren, see, and she says everyone should." Now my mother opened her mouth, but I rushed on. "And then Max said if Miss Laura was going to be my grandmother, he'd better help me out by being my grandfather."

"You don't need to be adopted," my mother said softly. "You have grandparents."

My heart nearly leaped out of my chest. It had to be a dream. It was impossible! "But your parents—"

"Your father has parents." She rested her hand on my knee.

"But Russell said—"

She interrupted me. "I'm not talking about Russell."

"My real dad?" Of course he must have parents, but my mom had never talked about them and so I'd assumed they weren't alive. "How come I've never met them? Did they divorce us, too?"

My mother swallowed hard. "No. I send them school pictures of you and David every year."

"Why don't they write to me? Why don't they visit

us?" I was beginning to wish she had never told me. *I'd rather have my adopted grandparents than real ones who don't want me,* I thought.

"Don't get the wrong idea," my mother said quickly. "They love both you and David. But they know you have a good home with Russell and me and they didn't want to interfere."

I had to think. It sounded like a pretty convenient excuse to me. But I had never known much about my parents' divorce. My father had left before I was born, and my mother never talked about him. Russell is the only father I've ever known.

"Would you believe me if I showed you pictures?"

"You have pictures?" Whether they loved me or not, I had to see my very own grandparents.

I followed my mother down the hall to her bedroom. She pulled a photo album off her closet shelf. We lay on the bed together while she flipped through the pages. Then she opened the book flat and slid it toward me.

"This is your Grandmother and Grandfather Harper. They sent these pictures last year, after their vacation in England."

If my mother had any more to say, I didn't hear it. I leaned over the photographs and studied them. I tried to see something in them that I could recognize. My grandfather had a nose like David's. I didn't see anything that looked like me, but that

was still better than having a nose like my grandfather and my brother!

"Could I write to them?" I asked finally. "Would
they want to get a letter from me?"

I held my breath until my mother said, "I'm sure
they would love it."

She took the album from me and began searching
through it. A worn envelope fell out of the book. My
mother handed it to me. "Here's their address."

I felt as if I were holding something delicate and
rare. The return address told me they lived in Phoenix, Arizona. I jumped off the bed and headed for my
own room.

"Where are you going?" my mother called after
me.

"To write a letter."

"Don't you have a biology test tomorrow?"

I slid to a stop on the wood floor in the hall. If I
wanted to pass that test, I knew I had to study. But
I couldn't wait until tomorrow to write to my grandparents. Sure, I'd lived for thirteen years not knowing them, but it didn't matter; I had to write to them
immediately.

"I'll make it a short letter, okay?"

"Sounds good to me. Go ahead."

If things worked out the way I hoped they would,
I'd have plenty of time to write longer letters in the
future. This was like a dream come true.

I was going to have grandmother stories to share with Julie and Allie! I couldn't wait to go back to Pine Villa and share my news with Miss Laura and Max. Of course, I wasn't going to dump them. Now I was going to have *two* sets of grandparents—my real ones and my adopted ones!

"Becky, is that you?" my mother called when I came home from school two weeks later.

"No, it's King Kong. I've come to tear apart your home." Who else was she expecting? I always got home at three-twenty-five.

"You've got mail on the front table."

I dropped my book bag on the floor. Normally, I would have been trying to guess about my mail, but my brain was on vacation. I had just taken the biology retest. Yes, I'd done such a bad job on my biology test that my teacher had let me take a make-up exam.

My brain snapped to attention when I saw the Phoenix address in the corner of the envelope. I had a letter from my grandparents! The handwriting was very neat, and on the back there was a bird sticker that said something about endangered animals. I peeled it off very carefully, knowing I was going to keep it forever.

Then I sat down on the floor, right on the very spot where I'd been standing. I couldn't waste time walking to a chair. Not when I was holding a letter from my grandparents!

I slid the letter out of the envelope. It was written on heavy blue paper. My grandmother's handwriting filled the whole front side of the page and half of the back.

Taking a deep breath, I read it. And then I read it again.

My mother came into the room, trying to act casual. "What does the letter say?"

Once I opened my mouth, I couldn't stop the words from tumbling out of it. "They were surprised to get my letter. And excited. They promised to send some new pictures in their next letter. I think we're going to be pen pals. And they want to see me!"

My mom wrapped her arms around me. I hugged her, too. When we each took a step back, I saw tears in her eyes. Her voice was husky when she whispered, "I'm so happy for you."

My own voice sounded strangely deep as I told her, "I'm happy, too."

"So what are you going to do now?" My mother knew I always had ideas.

"Check my calendar to see when I have a few days off school so I can visit them."

"When do you plan to go?" she asked, grinning.

I thought for a minute. "Winter would be nice. I'd

like to spend some time in Phoenix when it's all snowy here."

"That sounds smart."

Of course, I could go to Phoenix *before* winter vacation. In that case I'd have to skip a few days of school . . . and some biology classes. That was a sacrifice I was prepared to make. Trips out of Vermont, some time off school—this grandparent thing was going to be great.

I wondered if my grandmother would take me to the zoo and buy me a sweatshirt with a parrot on it. Or if she would have a living room full of old photographs. I wanted to find out, soon.

Winter vacation sounded too far away. I'd have to check my calendar. There just *had* to be some way I could meet my grandparents before Christmas.

Remember what I said about ideas? I'm never sure where they come from, and I never know when to expect them. So I'm just waiting. I know I'll find a way to make it super special when I meet my grandmother and grandfather for the first time!

SPECIAL PARTY TIP
Becky's "Tutti-Frutti Punch"

The great thing about this recipe is you don't have to always follow it exactly. You can play around with it a little, substituting different fruit juices. Just don't get too creative, and always sample your recipe. (Sometimes flavors that *sound* like they'd go together, don't. So don't use your guests as guinea pigs. Test it on yourself first!)

Shopping list: Cranberry juice cocktail
                     Pink lemonade
                     Apple juice
                     White grape juice
                     (For all fruit juices listed, you can use frozen or bottled.)
                     Ginger ale
                     2 or 3 apples
                     2 or 3 oranges

Mix all the juices together in a big punch bowl. Slice the oranges and the apples and toss them in as well. At the very last moment, stir in the ginger ale. (You add the ginger ale last so your punch doesn't go flat too quickly.) Your tutti-frutti punch is ready to serve.